I0722392

The Best Part of Her

An Unconditional Love Story

By
Asia Celeste Martin and Lefornia Martin

The Best Part of Her

ISBN: 978-1-955579-07-0

Publisher: Luminous Publishing
www.luminouspublishing.com

For bulk orders or other inquiries, email:
info@luminouspublishing.com

Created and Designed in the USA

Table of Contents

Introduction

Hello beautiful! Loving you is always the first step of self-care and self-love. Having a good read is also a piece of self-care. Whether it is an audio book, eBook, or physical book; relax and let your mind roam into a bliss. Thank you for purchasing our book and making it a part of your collection.

There are women in the world that clique best with the opposite sex and men that clique best with the opposite sex. *The Best Part of Her* opens up the confidence and appreciation of the opposite sex in friendship and meaning just that!

This book will build up your love for the characters, your love for Naomi and how she loves people. Time is of the essence and it goes by pretty fast during this love cycle. Naomi's friendships and new love will have to be crammed into limited time, but it will suffice for everyone. This book will teach you to enjoy those around you and love them while you have time.

Growing up, especially in high school, I had a couple of female best friends. It seemed like I always got along or related more to the male friends. It was never anything more than friendships and I loved it. Going into my adult life, I had maybe one best friend and no male friends but still, in the workplace I got along with males better. It was never to be sexual but simply casual. I always wondered if men would accept me having male best friends and nothing more. That would bring so much insecurity and trust issues that I chose to just continue with one best friend or none at all. My goal is to help build self-love and confidence in relationships so that couples do not feel insecure about the opposite sex being their partner's best friend.

It is beneficial to have healthy friendships outside of your relationship but will it make or break yours is the ultimate question? Building that trust takes time, and no, it is not for everyone. Therefore, take some time and read *The Best Part of Her*. See what you discover and enjoy getting to know the best of Naomi.

I challenge you to put that ego aside "this girl is crazy thinking I am going to have another woman around my man; saying that is his best friend!" Let this read broaden your horizon to loving everyone but discerning when someone is trying to harm or hinder your relationship.

You will notice this book is a total of seven chapters, for the number seven is a sign of completion. May this book help you feel the completeness you are seeking. Whether that is you finding yourself, a new love, your faith, etc.

Welcome to The Best Part of Her!

Chapter 1
Never for the Streets

"Welcome all to my grand opening! DJ Von cut the music for a moment! Thank you, you know you been by boy since middle school." Naomi shouts up to the DJ booth.

DJ Von nods and proceeds to slow the music down to smooth Jazz, "Of course beautiful!" The event planner dims the fluorescent track lights to a more intimate setting. The purple backdrop where Naomi stood turned to Vanessa Butterflies. The butterflies then flew across the screens, along the walls and ceiling.

The room is filled with fifty of Naomi's close friends and family. Her Vanessa dance girls are also in attendance. The smell of honeysuckles filled the room to give it a vibrant outdoor vibe, honey, and citrus, to be exact. Naomi is a mid-height, petite, caramel-tone woman. Her smile can lighten up an entire stadium. She wore a mermaid tale, satin Versace dress. The dress complimented her curves well. Her hair is in half up and half down curly style. She had white gold studs, a butterfly necklace, along with a butterfly clutch. The red bottom heels also had white gold butterfly jewels that dangled from her ankles. The fine clothes and jewels do not define her personality but the work she has put into her business. Naomi always believed in presenting herself well. You never know who is watching. That is one crucial point her mother taught her.

As she is standing there, family and friends are smiling back; excited to hear what Naomi has to say. Naomi continues with her opening speech. She walks along the well-polished hard wood floors. The screen begins to fade in and out with the words of her studio name and pictures of her and the dance girls.

"I want to welcome you all to my grand opening of Vanessa's Butterfly Dance Studio," Naomi exclaims excitedly.

Everyone claps and shouts with enthusiasm.

"Thank you! Thank you to everyone that has come out to celebrate my success. My name is Naomi Russell. I would not be here without my heavenly father and you all. I chose Vanessa Butterfly as the name of the studio because I love Australia and butterflies. In Australia, there are these beautiful creatures called Vanessa Butterfly. The purpose of the foundation name is to demonstrate to the public that the talent we have is as graceful and free as butterflies.

I had a troubled childhood. I had to spend time away from my mother. My home was an orphanage for a few months. Those months felt like years. I then lived with my father, who was my best friend. He passed away when I was ten. That shook my world. I came home and I had to regain my sanity. I could not have done that without the Lord, my friends, church family, and my mother. With that being said, even though life can feel like a rollercoaster that will never end, secure yourself and ride until you see the end. Remember that is just the end of that journey and another will begin. I thank God for the lessons I have learned. I had to go through the trials and tribulations to prepare me for moments like this. I felt as if I could not handle what life threw at me, but I am well equipped and ready now. I had to grow into the woman I am today. Throughout my teenage years, I was a force to be reckoned with. Nobody could tell me anything until I had a life-changing experience that showed me differently. I felt as if I had to check anybody that spoke down on me or looked at me side eyed. Thank you, Lord, for humility and much needed counseling. Mental health is wealth, you all. Do not ever hesitate to take your problems to the Lord and to a mental health professional that you feel comfortable with.

I am going to wrap up my speech so that we enjoy that amazing food and champagne over there. Tonight, not only are we celebrating the grand opening of Vanessa Butterfly, we are celebrating friendship and agape love. No matter a person's color, sexual orientation, beliefs, denomination, we are to love wholeheartedly. As many of you know, I have five best friends, and no, they are not the typical best friends a woman usually has. I would not trade them in if my life depended on it. They are all go-getters, pushing me to be the best woman I can be and vice versa. There is never a dull moment with them. "We push each other to be the best we can possibly be," Naomi happily states.

All of her best friends stand up throughout the studio, take a bow, and a seat back at their tables. As Naomi concludes her speech, everyone claps and congratulates Naomi's success.

Vanessa's Butterfly girls put on a performance for all guests in attendance. The track lights flicker with purple and yellow throughout the entire studio. Naomi makes her rounds to give thanks and express her gratitude to all that showed her love. Naomi's mother pulls Naomi to the side.

"Baby, do you have a moment? I would like to show you something." Oleatha questions.

"Right at this moment? Mother, I have a few more tables to get to before the guests start gathering their belongings to leave." Naomi explains as she turns her body to glance at the guests in the studio.

"It will only take a moment."

Oleatha gestures at the double door of the main entrance. In walks a tall, mocha-toned, slender woman. She glided like a contestant from the Next Top Model. She wore three-inch heels and a Versace gown that draped to the floor. Naomi completely turns around, and she knows exactly who the woman is. Although it has been over two and a half decades, she remembers that scar on the side of her eye.

Naomi walks up to the mysterious woman and throws her short arms around her. The woman hugs her in return. They both shed tears and rock each other until they are able to let go.

"Paige Sutton. Is it really you?"

"In the flesh, well, Paige Sutton-Naples. I's married now."

Naomi and Paige laugh. They love *The Color Purple,* the book and the movie. As children, they were very close, like Celie and Netty. Nothing could tear them apart. Paige stood up for Naomi when Naomi thought she did not have a voice.

All of the feelings and emotions that Naomi went to therapy for suddenly came rushing back to her. She thought she talked through all of the past hurt and pain. Losing Paige hurt her deeply.

Naomi started to turn pale in the face.

"May I have some water, please?" Naomi says as she sits down at one of the round tables for the guest.

"Darling, you do not look so good." Naomi hears a country accent speak to her.

Naomi is sweating profusely. Her eyes become blurry.

"I feel cold. Where is my father?"

Naomi falls to the floor. Everyone is shouting and astonished that Naomi has fallen ill.

Naomi lays there and her body is weak.

"Someone call 911! Ekon shouts into the crowd.

"On it. Come on, Javi." Flame yells back to Ekon. Flame and Javier run to the outside of the building so that they are prepared to let the EMT in to assist Naomi.

Her feet are extremely swollen." Ekon kicks into medical professional mode. Although his career is assisting animals, he majored in neurology and became a brain neurologist first.

Hunter is next to her, fanning Naomi, trying to decipher what she is saying as she mumbles in her slumber.

"Shhh, shhh, darling. Help is coming. This was a beautiful night. I guess you wanted the ending to be a bang. But you did not have to scare us like this."

"Daddy, where are you? Daddy, come on. We got to get out of here." Naomi mumbles.

"Sounds like she is talking about Hurricane Katrina." Enrique remembered that was one of the horrific moments in Naomi's life.

Oleatha and Paige scattered to locate pillows and a towel to help with the sweating. Also, a blanket for her chills.

"It seems to look as if she is suffering from a stroke." Ekon speaks with anguish.

"Oh my goodness, this is my fault. I knew I should not have come. This was too much for her. Plus, she lost her father a few years ago, and I was not there for her." Paige begins to cry on Oleatha.

"Honey, this is not your fault. Do not beat yourself up about this. You were a child and so was Naomi. If anyone should be held accountable for what she went through, it should be me. But you know what? This is not the time to do that. She needs us now. Naomi is sick and we have to help her get well.

Oleatha and Paige rush into the studio room and prop Naomi's feet up on pillows, placing the blanket over her body and the towel on her forehead.

Oleatha gathers all those who are still at the studio for prayer.

"Let us pray. Father God, Naomi is in need of your grace and mercy. We do not know what is going on in her body. Would you please hold her in your arms and let her know that she will be alright? That she is not alone and that you would never leave nor forsake her. We all know what she has been through, but the strength that she possesses comes from you and you alone. Cover my baby, Lord God. Whatever this is, I know you are the ultimate healer, and you will deliver her. In Jesus's name, let us all say. Amen!"

Everyone says amen in agreement to the prayer.

The EMT and fire fighters arrive. Flame and Javier guide them through the double-door entrance.

Naomi is mumbling continuously as the paramedics approach her.

"We know she is unconscious, but they have to ask. What is your name?"

Naomi mumbles and is unable to answer the question.

"Do you know what year it is?"

Still no response.

"Last question. Do you know where you are right now?"

Naomi was not able to answer any of the questions.

"It is too early to say, but she may have suffered a stroke. We will load her up in the ambulance and get her to the nearest emergency room. Who wants to ride with her?"

"I will. I am her mother." Oleatha grabs her purse and Naomi's.

"Come on, baby. You are coming with me." Oleatha grabs Paige's hand.

"Boys, you all get home safely, and I will update you as soon as I know something."

"Alright mama. Let us know if you need us to come on down there tonight." Hunter assures Mama Oleatha.

Oleatha and Paige walk out the main entrance and get into the back of the ambulance rig. The ambulance drives away to the Christian Memorial Hospital South.

As the ambulance drives away, the guys stand in the middle of the street with disbelief, anguish, and confusion on their faces.

"So we are not going to talk about the fine friend Naomi never told us about?" Jokes Enrique.

"Look man, this is not the time for you to be playing and trying to flirt with Naomi's childhood friend. She needs all the prayers she can get right now." Ekon interjects.

"For sho, you know I am going to pray for our sister. I am just saying. She never told us about her. Flame, aren't you her oldest friend? How did you not know about her?

"Y'all already know Naomi, and I came up from a group home, and we were almost teenagers. This goes back, way back when Ms. Oleatha was struggling with keeping Naomi. Before Naomi had to live with her father." Flame explains.

"Well y'all, I am going to get Nubia home. I know this all frightens her. Her Godmother getting sick is the last thing my little lady needs right now." Hunter walks back into the building, kneeling to help little Nubia get her shawl on. He runs his hands through her curly and thick locks.

"Daddy. I am scared for Naomi. Is she going to be alright?' Nubia looks up to her father with curiosity in her eyes.

"You know what, Nubia? I am not sure. But our God is the ultimate healer. Let us do what we can and pray that she pulls through this. We will let God do his job and heal her body. How does that sound?

Nubia grabs her father's hand and nods slowly, up and down. She walks out of the building and waves at all of her uncles; Enrique, Ekon, Javier, and Flame.

Naomi arrives to Christian Memorial Hospital South, stable but not alert. The bright lights are making her sick to her stomach. She is immediately taken to an emergency room. In the waiting area, Oleatha, Paige, and the bishop from their Cathedral awaited news. Bishop Rutherford of Mount Sinai prayed with Oleatha and Paige. They prayed without ceasing. They prayed until the physician on call that night came with an update. The physician stood tall and he grabbed Oletha's hands. They were cold. Oleatha looked up at the physical and said, "What is the diagnosis, doctor? Is my child alright?"

Bishop Rutherford and Paige put their hands on her shoulder for comfort. The physician looked at Paige and Bishop Rutherford and finally at Oleatha.

"Ms. Russell, my name is Dr. Parker O'Brien. I am the doctor that is overseeing Naomi's care. Naomi is stable." The physician assures everyone.

"Oh thank the Lord!" Paige yells out with praise.

"Yes, yes. Thank you, Father." Bishop Rutherford is pleased with the report.

Oleatha observes in the doctor's eyes that there is more.

"Well doctor, that is the good news you gave us. What is the bad news?"

Doctor O'Brien stands up tall which makes Oleatha have to look even further up at him.

The symptoms that Naomi experienced tonight: the dizziness, cold sweats, feeling overheated, the slurring speech are all signs of stroke."

"Oh Lord. She is only thirty-four. She has so much life ahead of her." Oleatha begins to cry. She pulls her cloth out of her clutch and wipes her tears. She is able to pull herself together to hear more of what the doctor has to say.

"Now, Ms. Russell. I can tell you are a woman of faith. Keep the prayers and positive thoughts going for Naomi. She needs them right now. Try to get some rest if you can. Let us help determine what is going on with her body. We are going to run a few more tests. But you all are sure welcome to go into the room and see her. It will be a few more hours until she has an assigned room. She is currently in room seven. Are there any questions you all have for me?" Dr. O'Brien asks before going back to the physician's station.

Oleatha shakes her head no as she gathers the information the doctor delivered to her.

"No, no, thank you, doc. We will be sure to look after Sister Russell and get her back there to see Sister Naomi."

"Alright, I am here until seven o'clock in the morning, but if you have any questions, just holler." Dr. O'Brien reassures.

"Yes sir." Agrees Paige.

Paige, Bishop Rutherford and Oleatha make their way down the hall. Room seven is at the very end of the hall. Bishop Rutherford approaches the room door first. They know not to knock because Naomi is unable to answer at the moment. Paige is holding Oleatha's hand. Oleatha has a dazed look on her face.

"Mama, you sure you are ready to go in? You do not have to if you are not yet comfortable." Paige questions.

"I must. Naomi needs me more than she ever has right now. I was not the best mother to her, so I am going to be that and more to her. I am ready to go in." Oleatha confirms.

Bishop pushes the door open. The room is dark. The only light in the room was from the bathroom, which the door was cracked. Also, from the hospital computer which displayed 'Christian Memorial Hospital.' The room was very chilly, however Naomi had a thick white blanket that covered her body.

Oleatha walked past Bishop Rutherford and Paige. She touched Naomi's blanket and the cover was warm to the touch. She sheds a tear and thinks about how vulnerable her child is. No mother ever wants to see their child in this much pain.

"Bishop, can we please pray one more time for her?" Oleatha asks as she stares at Naomi from the bed side.

"We can pray as many times as we need, Sis." Bishop Rutherford assures.

Bishop Rutherford walks to the other side of Naomi's bed. He holds his left hand out to grab Oleatha's hand and his right hand out to welcome Paige to prayer. Paige walks over and grabs both Bishop and Oleatha's hand. The prayer circle is now formed.

"Oh Lord, our heavenly father. We come to you in declaration. We now know what Naomi is battling and with your healing power, she will be healed. Naomi is not in this battle alone. We will continue to lift her up in prayer until she is fully recovered. Until whatever this condition is, is removed or controlled. The devil will not have this child. She has much more work to do on this Earth. You and only you know the day and the hour, but this is not her time Lord. Strengthen her right now. Work on her mind while she is resting. Prepare her for whatever assignment she is heading to next. Give her the guidance. Be her beacon in darkness. Right now, Lord!"

"Right now." Paige whispers.

"Help her mother keep her strength throughout this difficult time. A parent should not ever see their child hurt like this. But we know everything happens for a reason. Sister Naomi will have a testimony after this experience. Help her, Lord."

"Help her." Paige and Oleatha says in agreement.

"Help her Lord. In Jesus precious name. Amen!" Everyone says, "Amen." Even Naomi.

Oleatha lets the Bishop's and Paige's hand go immediately. She sits on Naomi's bed and holds her left hand in both of her hands.

"Naomi, can you hear me? It is your mother baby."

"Yes." Naomi answers slow and softly. With her eyes closed and clinched tight.

"My head mama." Naomi lifts her left hand and places it on her forehead. She can feel the cold I.V. on her hand against her head.

"Where am I?"

"The hospital." Paige replies.

"Do you remember what happened?' Oleatha questions.

"I, I, remember the studio grand opening but not anything after." Naomi confirms.

"Well, you started getting ill while talking to Paige. Then fainted. You were unconscious for some time so the paramedics rushed you here to Christian Memorial." Oleatha explains.

Naomi is able to open one eye and look over at her mother. Then over at Bishop Rutherford. Lastly, at Paige.

"Paige. Where did you come from? I have not seen you since we were kids."

"I came towards the end of the grand opening. We talked briefly before your episode. But I am here now. We have more than enough time to catch up. Just get better, hun." Paige reassures Naomi.

"I am going to send a group text to the guys, you know they are worried about you. And poor Nubia was so distraught." Oleatha explains to Naomi.

"Oh, I am so sorry she had to see that. She has been through so much. This is the last thing she needed." Naomi continues.

"HEY FELLAS! QUICK UPDATE. NAOMI IS AWAKE AND TALKING WITH US RIGHT NOW. I WILL HAVE YOU ALL OVER FOR BREAKFAST IN THE MORNING TO EXPLAIN WHAT IS GOING ON. BUT ALL IS WELL. LOVE, MAMA." She includes prayer hands and heart emoji's.

Hunter immediately replies back. "Oh thank the Lord. I am going to tell Nubia now. Thanks Ma!"

Then Javier, "Gracias a Dios!"

"I know God had her covered. I will see you all in the morning. Thank you, mama." Ekon replies.

"That's what's up. God is good. Thanks ma duke." Flame responds back."

A few minutes later Enrique replies. " I was worried mama. I know the Lord does not want us to have fear in our hearts but I was truly scared. Thank you for the good news."

"So, all the fellas are ecstatic you are well. Hunter is updating Nubia now. I invited them over tomorrow for breakfast to let them know more about what is going on." Oleatha states.

"Mama, what is going on. You have yet to tell me what is going on with my body. Are you all hiding something from me?" Naomi looks at everyone with somber in her eyes.

"Baby." Oleatha muttered out. She begins to cry. Bishop Rutherford stands next to Oleatha and comforts her. Paige is able to deliver the news to Naomi. She walks to Naomi's bedside and adjusts her pillows, then she caresses her hair with her hand.

"Naomi, Doctor O'Brien came and spoke with us earlier. He informed us that your body gave signs of a stroke; which caused you to faint at the grand opening. They are running test and they should be back sometime soon and hopefully we will know more about what caused this and how to move forward. But you know you are a strong sister." Paige explains.

Naomi stares at the wall in front of her and absorbs the prognosis, as of right now what is going on in her body is unknown. Naomi does not cry but she is quiet for approximately seven minutes.

"Well, all I can do is just be positive and pray right?" Naomi smiles and looks at her mother, Bishop, and her friend.

"Exactly." Paige agrees as she looks at Bishop Rutherford and Oleatha.

Then suddenly Naomi begins to murmur once again, as she did at the grand opening. Her eyes rolled to the back of her head, her head falls over to the left, and her body shakes repeatedly.

Paige dashes over to the call light that is on Naomi's legs. Bishop runs out of the room as fast as he can and yells, "Nurse, somebody help. We need help right now!"

Oleatha falls to the middle of the floor. After Paige pushes the red emergency button, she runs over to Naomi. The nurses run in and demands everyone to stand back. Paige helps Oleatha off of the floor to the chair in the far corner. The nurses lye Naomi's bed flat. They remove all objects from her bed. They do not control or restrain her movements. The nurses stay by Naomi's side until the seizure surpasses. One nurse is staring at the clock, timing how long the seizure lasts. Another is at the foot of the bed with fear in her eyes, as if she is training. Finally, the seizure passes. The nurses observe Naomi's body to make sure her body is alright. Also, to ensure there are no physical, neurological complications.

"As of now, Naomi is stable. The results will be arriving from the lab anytime now. We have also called Dr. O'brien to come to the room. He is going to be leaving soon, but he will make it his priority to stop by her room first." The nurse explains to everyone.

"Oh please, have him stop by as soon as he can. Something is going on in her body, something that she has never went through. We need answers now, nurse. I mean right now!" Oleatha screams.

"Alright, now." Bishop Rutherford interjects.

"Of course, she is very upset nurse. This child here is her only. Please have the doctor come in immediately. We do need answers." Bishop explains to the nurse.

"I do understand. No need to apologize, I would be the same way about my own child. Please believe me when I say, we are going to do everything in our power to figure this out." The nurse grabs both of Oleatha hands and embraces her with a hug. She then turns and nods at Bishop Rutherford and Paige. Finally, proceeds to the room door, pushes the hand sanitizer dispenser, and walks out. The fellow nurses follow suit.

Naomi begins to mumble faint words again.

"My broth. My, my."

"Your what, Naomi?" Bishop Rutherford walks over to the bedside.

Oleatha remains seated in her chair. She is unable to stand from the events that just unfolded. Paige continues to rub her back.

"My brothers." Naomi completes the phrase.

Naomi then has a flashback to the year 2016.

She remembers the amazing time she had with her five best friends at club Dubai, five years ago. Naomi looked the same from five years ago to present day. All of the fellas have changed but not significantly. Hunter and Naomi walk to the club waiting line, where there are over two dozen people waiting to get in. The music can be heard outside and it was bumping. People all around were anticipating the wait, but Hunter was ready to go before getting inside.

"Elizabeth made meatloaf, potatoes, and steamed string beans tonight. I am glad I ate something before we got here. You know I do not hold liquor well." Hunter rambles on.

"Well you should have brought Liz along because we know you are going to babysit your drink tonight." Enrique laughs.

"Here you go. Always want to clown somebody, when you the whole clown. I mean the main attraction." Ekon defends Hunter.

"Thanks partner." Hunter thanks gratefully and laughs hysterically.

"I wonder if Flame has arrived yet? He said he would be able to get us in before midnight because the price is going to double." Naomi questions as she pulls out her phone to text him.

"Where you at, dude?

We been standin' out here for 30 minutes."

It really has only been five minutes, but that will speed the progress up.

"Por ahi!" Javier exclaims in Spanish.

"Donde." Naomi replies.

"Aqui misma."Flame shouts back.

"Mismo" Javier corrects Flame.

"Misma, Mismo, let's get some Mimosa's!" Flame shouts.

Flame leads the crew out of the waiting line and through the club doors. The music grows louder and people are dancing everywhere. The club was very hot from the constant movement, but that did not stop the excitement. Naomi and Flame are walking and dancing all the way to their private booth. Flame had champagne waiting at the table and did not pop it until they arrived. Each of them had a glass. Flame and Naomi then made their way to the dance floor. The two of them were back and forth from the dance floor to the booth majority of the night. Ekon sat at the table all night texting away and the look of worry was on his face. Enrique sat at the one that was lit up with colors on the marble stand. He conversed with women at the bar and many of them turned him down. He was very uptight, but he has corny jokes. Javier stayed seated at the booth as well, just smiling away. He was definitely enjoying himself, watching everyone dance, talk, and mingle. Javier was intimidated by the culture. His English is not fluent, but it is progressing. Hunter sat at the bar as well, texting Liz. He then FaceTimed her and took the call outside so that he could wish his queen and princess a goodnight.

Nubia got on the phone first. Her curly hair is all over her head. She wore a pink Princess Tiana pajama dress. Elizabeth sat behind her with an adult size Princess Tiana Dress.

"Daddy, you having fun tonight. Mama said you are with Auntie Naomi. Can I talk to her?

"Well baby, Auntie Naomi is inside with your uncles. They are having all the fun. Looks like you and mommy are having even more fun. You got mommy to break out here Princess dress."

"Yeah, she did, daddy. Will you play dress up with me when you get home?"

"I will, Nubia, well not right when I get home. You will be sound asleep."

"Okay, daddy. I love you. Handshake."

Nubia and Hunter do their handshake over the video. Elizabeth smiled from ear to ear to see her husband and daughter bond so well together.

"Alright, Nubia. Off you go. I will be in your room is a moment. Just going to chat with daddy for a moment."

Nubia blows Hunter a kiss and kisses Elizabeth as well and dashes out of their room. You can hear her little feet race down the hall through the phone.

"Having fun, baby. I know you just sitting around. Get out there and bust some moves." Liz cracks up laughing.

"No baby, you know I cannot dance without you being here."

"See, I should have went in your place. It would have been nice to have a night out. I love you, Hunt."

"I love you more, Liz. When I get home, I am going to curl up with you and hold you until Nubia runs in and forces us out of bed."

"Sounds good, baby. Alright, I will let you go. Have fun and be safe. God bless."

"God bless you too, my queen."

Hunter stood against the brick wall outside the club for a moment and soaked up the joy he received from his baby girl and wife. He pushed his red hair back and walked tall into the club. He walked back in dancing, sat at the booth.

"You must be on the phone with the fam?" Enrique questions.

"Yeah, that is my babies." Hunt says with a huge smile.

"Yeah, someday I will have Mrs. Right and my little army." Enrique hopefully says.

"You will man, just give it time and let God do his work. He who finds a wife, finds a good thing." Hunter quotes.

"John 18:12. Exactly what I been praying for. Being an overworked accountant, I am not sure if that will happen no time soon."

Naomi and Flame come rushing back to the table like two big children. They sit down for a moment.

"Y'all seriously came just to sit at the booth all night? See I could have rented this out to some big ballers." Flame says.

"Really Flame, the time with your friends is not more important?" Ekon questions as he places his phone down and folds his hands into each other.

"Y'all know I love y'all, but dang, live a little. Dang!"

Naomi jumps up out of her seat as she hears the introduction to her favorite pop song playing throughout the club.

"Aye, aye, aye, now you know this is my song! Twin get over here, let's show them how we do it!"

"Say less best friend, let's GO!" Flame shouts.

Flame is Naomi's party friend. He is also her twin flame. They share the same birthday. Same month, day, and year. Flame and Naomi met in a group home. Flame is also a dance instructor, more so choreographer. He is the top choreographer in the Midwest. He stands 6'5" and weighs no more than 160 pounds and can dress his behind off. His go to fit, which he is wearing tonight is: a red bottom fedora, satin shirt, and skinny suit paints. He had curly, cold black hair, that was shaped in a bald fade mohawk. Naomi loved how he carried himself and how he was the life of the party. He did not care about what anyone thought of him.

Naomi stops Flame, "Hold on a sec, we got to get the rest of the guys so they can see this!" Flame went through a tough time growing up, but he made it through the trials and tribulations. Naomi wanted him to be more dedicated to the Lord, but she knew she had some growth as well.

Naomi runs to the seating area and reaches out, "Hunt, Rique, Javi, Ekon, come on, you know you can't miss this!"

"Alright, Naomi you and Flame got fifteen minutes and I got to get back to the house with to Elizabeth and Nubia." Hunter says briskly. As he gestures to the front door.

Rique, Javi, and Ekon shake their heads in agreement.

"I mean, we have been here all night and y'all been dancing the whole time." Enrique points.

Naomi overhears a group of women gossiping and discussing what they think she is doing with all the guys.

"You know one of them is hitting that, nah I bet it is all of them. Shoot I do not blame her though." The woman giggles.

Before Naomi meets Flame at the dance floor, she gracefully walks over to their table and says, "See the difference between me and y'all, I do not need to open my legs for attention."

The guys pull her away. Naomi did not take no mess when it comes to her and the fellas. The guys already knew to get her out while they are ahead.

"I'm cool, I'm cool. Javi come on, you can let me go." Naomi reassures.

Javier lets Naomi go and agrees and let go.

"Alright, you say so; I let go." He says in his broken English.

Naomi turns around smoothly, "On second thought, I got something else to say."

She squeezes in between the other women.

"Excuse me ladies. Nothing about me is basic or simple minded. No I do not have daddy issues. These men are my brothers. I know y'all might use that term loosely with your boyfriends to cover up your lil side pieces. Or what is the new one? " Naomi questions.

"Sneaky link." Enrique mumbles.

"Yessss. Sneaky link. But these men here, nah, it's non of that. They got me till the wheels fall off and they know I will do the same. Can you say the same about these ladies? I advise you to re-evaluate yourself and your situation before judging mine." Naomi checks the group of women.

All the women look astonished and in disbelief that she confronted them and shut down their petty conversation.

After Naomi felt wrong for the way she handled that situation, she questioned why she circled around to confront them and she could have just turned the other cheek.

She can see Flame rocking back and forth, dancing to their song.

"Come on Nam, this your part. Let's get it."

Naomi rushes to the dance floor and demand the DJ Von to play "Walk It Out" by DJ Unk. Naomi proceeds with her signature move and she flips backward. Flame and Naomi steals the attention of everyone in the club. Hitting the early 2000's moves. Once she and Flame finishes dancing, they gather up the guys and head to the front of the venue.

Naomi is still bothered by her response. It was not the most appropriate answer, but she wanted others to know it was simply true love for her brothers. No intimate relationships. There were no hidden emotions. These men care for her like a sister and best friend. From that moment, Naomi knew she needed to heal from the past hurt and pain. Naomi needed to heal and not let small things trigger her. She always kept the phrase "what would Jesus do?" In the front of her mind. It is more than just a popular phrase. What would Jesus really do? Jesus would turn the other cheek. Jesus would never leave nor forsake others. He would love his enemies. He would love wholeheartedly unconditional love. Jesus would put his needs before others. That sounds too good to be true, that sounds perfect to be exact. Although, none of us are perfect; we can walk a more righteous life. A purposeful life. A life believing that God gave his only begotten son, that whoever shall believe in him; will have everlasting life. Naomi knew all of these things but life tested her. People pulled the dark out of her.

Naomi remains unconscious from the present-day seizure. She can hear the faint whispers of her loved ones and doctors. She still cannot pull herself out of the trance. It felt as if her body was paralyzed but her mind was going.

Naomi's mind then flashes back to when Hunter was the most vulnerable.

It is now the year 2019 and Naomi arrives to Hunter's home, which he shared with Elizabeth and their daughter. Naomi gets out of her car and her feet are hurting from the walking around at the office. She stops by every other day to check on Hunter and Nubia. She walks around her SUV and looks around the outside. The grass is extremely tall and turned brown plants that Elizabeth planted, but had not been watered. The birdhouse was now empty due to the birds no longer sticking around. Naomi inputs her key to Hunter's home and pushes one of the double doors open.

"Hunter? Hunter? I know you are home." Naomi's voice echoed throughout the vestibule.

"Today is going to be a better day. Get up Hunt." Naomi pleads with Hunter.

Naomi walks down the hall and up to the wide, hardwood steps. Hunter and Elizabeth's room is the first room off of the steps to the right.

Naomi knocks on the door and no response. She proceeds with opening the door slowing and peaking her head in. Hunter is laying in his California king size bed in his massive suite. Hunter is Naomi's best friend. He is from Texas and moved to Saint Louis with his late wife Elizabeth. Elizabeth passed away from stage four breast cancer two years ago. She had such a beautiful soul. Elizabeth had the most beautiful dark skin and that is why Hunter fell in love with her. He could not take his eyes off of her silky skin and naturally curly hair. He loved how pure her heart was and how she loved to help any and everyone. They have a daughter who is Naomi's God daughter, Nubia. Hunter is spicy white, a Caucasian person that preference is the African-American ethnicity. A person who got some soul in 'em. Hunter has more soul than Elizabeth. That is what Liz use to say. Hunter put a pause on his career as a CEO of the largest investment firm in world to be a full-time father to Nubia. He is now a full-time stay at home nanny. All the children love him and the parents love him even more. He is beyond patient and understanding.

"Naomi, I am going to get up, I just need about 10 more minutes!" Hunter exclaims in his country voice. Curled up with the family picture.

"Not happening today Hunt, we have a brunch scheduled. Plus we still have to take Nubia to the stylist, look at my baby hair." Naomi and Nubia laughs.

"Look at her gosh, I don't know how to do my own baby hair. Liz always took great care of her. It is like I was present but I wasn't there." Hunter begins to cry.

"You can't beat yourself up Hunt. You were a great husband and you are a great father to this day. Do you think this is what Liz would want you to do?" Naomi questions Hunter.

"No." Hunter gently yells out.

"Do you think this is what the Lord would want you to do?"-Naomi

"God no! Okay Naomi. I will get up so we can get going. You are always there for me." Hunter agrees.

"That is what best friends are for. Alright stop it before we are both sitting here crying all day." Naomi chuckles jokily.

Nubia dashes back into the suite and jumps on the California king bed.

"Daddy, Daddy! Auntie Naomi! Are we leaving now?" Nubia laughs excitedly.

All three of them laughs hysterically.

"Yes baby girl, you are right on time. How about that handshake?" Hunter tickles Nubia.

Nubia and Hunt do their secret handshake.

"Oh so yall just gonna leave your girl out like that, I see how it is!" Naomi jokes as her and Nubia walks out the room.

Hunter gets himself together for the day. Nubia and Naomi walk down the steps, through the long hallway and out the double doors to the SUV. They wait while Hunter locks the doors to his home grabs Nubia's booster seat out of his Audi A3 sedan. Naomi unlocks her SUV with her thumb against the door handle. Before Hunt can click the booster to the car seat, Nubia hopped in through the other door.

"I got it daddy, now come on get in the car." Nubia continues to fasten the seat belt around her body. Naomi drives around the circle driveway and makes their way to the hair stylist.

"God mommy, may you please play Deliver Me (This Is My Exodus)? I love that song."

"Sure baby, you trying to get a praise break going this fine Saturday morning!" Naomi shouts.

Deliver me begins to play and Nubia is in the back seat, singing her heart out. Her curly soft hair is swaying back and forth. Hunter is looking out the window with his grey cardigan on, arms folded, and hands tucked under his arm, humming softly.

"So Hunter, what style you think Nubia should get this time? Last time she got a blow out and twisted updo." Naomi interrupts his daydreaming.

"Hmm, well um. I love it when she gets the silk press like you suggested earlier. It shows off her beautiful face structure." Hunter smiles and looks back at his Nubia.

Nubia continues to sing the song, hitting all the notes, and she smiles back at her father. Naomi looks at her through the rearview mirror. The gospel music continues to play and they sing songs together. Naomi pulls up to the salon. Mrs. Dee, the salon owner, is waiting on Nubia. She waves at Hunter and Naomi. Hunter gets out of the front passenger door and opens the door for Nubia. Nubia hops out and is now excited to get her hair done.

"Is Mrs. Dee doing my hair daddy? I love her." Nubia questions excitedly. Mrs. Dee styled Nubia and Elizabeth's hair every two weeks. Not as often now that Elizabeth is gone and Hunter is now learning to take care of Nubia on his own.

"Yes darling. She is going to get that hair looking fried, dyed, and laid to the side." Hunter jokes in his country voice.

"Oh goodness do not say that again." Naomi jokes as she is now standing next to Nubia.

"Nubia, Honey be good. Do not give Mrs. Dee a hard time saying you are tender headed to get out of getting your hair detangled." Naomi mentions to Nubia.

"Yes ma'am!" Nubia agrees.

"Love you Nubia, see you soon!" Hunter says as he blows Nubia a kiss.

Nubia blows a kiss back and holds Mrs. Dee's hand as they walk back into the salon.

Moments later, Hunter and Naomi arrive at Jed Muddy Uptown Dining Cafe downtown Saint Louis for brunch. The cafe had some of the best coffee in the Midwest, actually in competition with Starbucks.

Hunter unbuckles his seat belt and gets out of the front seat passenger side and now opens the door for Naomi. He is such a gentlemen and Elizabeth knew she had one of the finest men out there. As they walk into the cafe, he is still anxious and his body language projected nervousness. Naomi rubbed his back for reassurance and security. Hunter opens the cafe door and the workers greeted them from afar, knowing that Hunter and Naomi are regulars. They proceed to their favorite table, Naomi sits down on one side, and Hunter on the other.

"I know you have not ate as of yet; take a look at the menu Hunter. Take your time. I am going to go to the ladies room for a moment."

"Alright Naomi. Thank you."

Naomi goes to the restroom which is not far away in the compact diner. As she walks into the restroom, she thinks about what to talk about with Hunter. He is not as talkative as he was since Elizabeth died.

"Just be natural Naomi, this is your best friend. Lord give me the words to help encourage Hunter. He needs you and Nubia needs her father to pull through."

She looks up at the mirror and smiles, then washes her hands and grabs paper towels to dry her hands. She grabs the door with the paper towels and throw them in the trashcan next to the door. When she returns to the table, Hunter had water ordered for both of them, coffee for Naomi, and tea for himself.

"Thanks Hunt. So, you think about what you want to eat? Cause I am starving."

"I will get the Egg Benedict. I am not too hungry, you know."

"Okay, well at least you are eating something. I am going to go with the biscuit and gravy with a side of turkey sausage."

The waiter arrives to their table and takes their order. Naomi and Hunter sit quietly for a moment. Hunter begins the conversation with appreciation.

"Naomi, you know I questioned God when he took Elizabeth. I thought she would be here with me forever. Now I know not literally forever but at least to see Nubia grow up to an adult. We have more children and their children have children. We spoil our grandkids and send them back home so our kids can tell us not to do that again."

Hunter chuckles and Naomi laughs with him.

"I know I should not have questioned God but I was so in love with Elizabeth. She was my good thing, I would go to war for her. I just could not fight the battle of cancer for her. But why, why did she leave so soon?" Hunter sheds a tear and wipes it away with a napkin.

"Hunter, God understands your heart. You are not questioning him out of hatred, he knows how much you love Liz. But we know everything happens for a reason. We are all here for a season and this was the end to Liz's season. I know it does not sit well with you and I cannot truly know how it feels. I love her too Hunt. It is alright to grieve and have questions for God. Just do not let those questions turn into hate. When I lost my dad, my whole world turned upside down. I wanted to know why God took him and I was literally right down the street from him. Maybe I could have saved him. But how when he worked on an oil rig? There is not any service to call him and tell him the hurricane is heading his way. Somethings are just out of our control. Liz's cancer is out of your control." Naomi states as she empathizes with Hunter.

"But if I was around more, instead of working like a mad man. I worked hard because I did not want our family to struggle. My family struggled when I was a child and did a darn good job covering it up. I did not want that for my family. I planned to work hard for a few years so we could enjoy the fruits of my labor. Instead I missed learning my child, and knowing my wife was dying."

"Hunter, you stayed with Liz day and night. You went to every radiation session. You sat with her through the chemo. You cut your head bald when she lost her hair. You made sure Nubia was at every event and recital. Liz adored that, she knew you are a good man. What you can do now, is be a father to Nubia. Show her that even though we lose ones that we love, take time to grieve and heal. Then get back up and keep going with life. Remember Liz at every moment. Just know she is sitting with God and looking down on us. You have to be here for Nubia and I mean, physically, emotionally, mentally, and socially. God will guide you through, just keep your faith.

"I am trying and I will keep trying. I do need the Lord to guide me through this. I feel so lost at times. I know Nubia needs me to be here for her. Gosh, I need her more than anything."

The food arrives hot and fresh from the kitchen.

"Any refills on the drinks?" The waiter asks.

"Yes, please. I would like more coffee." Naomi passes her cup to the waiter.

Hunter shakes his head no. "No thank you."

They pray over their food silently and begin eating. The waiter returns with Naomi's coffee. Once they are done with their breakfast, Naomi goes to pull out her wallet to pay.

"What are you doing? No ma'am, put that up. I will not have you paying and you know that." Hunter says seriously.

Naomi laughs because the look on Hunter's face is very serious but he is legit serious. He would never let Elizabeth pay or anyone that he invited out in that matter.

"Okay Hunter, go for it. I will not stop you. I just add more to my tithe on Sunday. Thank you, Brother Hunt." Naomi continues to joke.

Hunter looks back at Naomi and laughs along with her. They both walk up to the dining bar and to the cash register. The waiter cashes the bill out for Hunter and he leaves her a generous tip. Both Naomi and Hunter walk to the door and Hunter opens the door for Naomi, she walks out, and to the SUV. Hunter is now walking with his hands unfolded and he also took the cardigan off. It is as if a weight was lifted off his shoulders.

"You know I actually have thought about being a stay-at-home dad, you know so I can give more time to Nubia."

"That is a great idea Hunt, I think she will love that." Naomi agrees as she pays attention to the traffic. Downtown can be very hectic in Saint Louis, especially during baseball or hockey games.

"I am also considering opening up a daycare service. My home is big enough."

"Wait. What? A daycare? You sure Hunt? Now that may be a bit much right now."

"I feel this is my calling. I can homeschool Nubia. I will more than likely start off with half days because I do not want to pull her from her friends. But many of the neighbors in my division complain how expensive the childcare is for them. I sure nuff' have enough money to survive and not charge out the wazoo. I will be helping many families. I want to make it where parents are not just working to cover childcare expenses. I want them to be able to see their children and families. I wish I would of then, that time." Hunter explains.

"You know Hunt. That is a wonderful idea. At first, I was a bit hesitant, but you are right. Even families who do have financial security need assistance from time to time. In addition, you are a passionate and trustworthy guy. All the neighbors love you, and I believe they will support you. Time to get your 'Daddy Day Care' started!" Naomi shouts out with laughter.

"Naomi, you are always cracking jokes. Got to love you."

Naomi arrives at the salon. Hunter and Naomi walk inside to pick up Nubia from the stylist. They admire her soft, thick, and lengthy pressed hair. Every coil was now laid and manageable. Hunter can now try natural styles that Liz would do to Nubia's hair. They tell her how beautiful she is and how she looks like her mother.

"Now what do you tell Mrs. Dee, Nubia?" Hunter asks.

"Thank you, Mrs. Dee, for doing my hair. I really like my hair." Nubia then runs to the door.

"Yes, thank you, Dee. You always deliver. I do not know what I would do without you." Hunter hugs Dee and walks over to Nubia.

"Dee, you did an amazing job. You know I will be coming to you soon." Naomi says.

"Whenever you are ready. I am here, lady."

Once Naomi takes Hunter and Nubia home, she drives to her home, which is about five minutes south of Hunter's home. When she pulls up to her loft, she parks in her designated parking spot. She gets out of the SUV and locks the door with her thumb on the door handle. She checks each door to make sure each door is locked. That is extra safety she takes, especially with living alone. Naomi then walks up to her main loft entrance and uses the scan card of her keyring to get into the building. She waves at the security guard. She rides the gated elevator to her door. She pushes the elevator door up and walks into her loft. She sits on her counter for a moment and reflects on the day, rubbing her toes. Then walks into her bathroom and begins her nightly routine. She puts her hair up into a bun and places a headband on the front of her hair. She enters her standup shower and lets the hot water run down her body. She feels the relaxation enter her body. She exfoliates her body and scrubs the day off. After her shower is complete, she flosses and brushes her teeth. She dries her mouth and begins washing her face and also exfoliates. She oils her body with baby oil. She then walks out of her bathroom in her yellow and purple plush rob. She lays across her bed and turns on smooth jazz. Naomi rolls across the bed to her nightstand and pulls out her Bible to begin her one-on-one time with the Lord. She reads the word on building a friend up during tough times.

She gets down on her knees and prays.

Naomi walks out of her room to the kitchen and grabs a glass to get cold water from the refrigerator. Once the water is gone, she walks back to her room and sits in the bay window on her daybed for a while, looking at the stars and moon. Naomi climbs in bed, she tosses and turns for a while. She finds it hard to get comfortable and go to sleep. Naomi has a deadline at work. She is a publisher for the largest magazine company in Saint Louis. For a while, Naomi has had writer's block or just nothing worth writing about.

Suddenly, a cold sweat comes over Naomi. She becomes dizzy and her eyes are blurry. Naomi thinks to herself, "I hope this is not the flu.' She instantly goes to her medicine cabinet and gets Father John. It is the most disgusting medicine.

She holds her nose and chugs it like she did as a child.

"It gets the job done!" Naomi laughs. That is what her father always said.

Naomi finally falls asleep and sleeps very well. The weird symptoms are even diminished. She gets herself ready for work.

Naomi grabs her coffee, heads to her garage, and gets into her Audi SUV. She drives to the magazine company she works for. She parks in her designated parking in the garage, walks into the office building and gets on the elevator. As she gets off at level 7, her boss instantly pops up behind her.

"OO-OOP!" Maggie calls out.

"So Naomi, what is going on? Any luck on a poppin' article for the magazine." Maggie says jokily.

"I do not know if the young people say popping anymore, Maggie. Come on, you know I am great at what I do, I will have an article soon. Just give me time." Naomi says as she continues to walk to her office.

"Alright, Naomi. I will give you a few more months!" She says demandingly.

Maggie always tries to be hard on Naomi, but truly she would be lost without her there at the company.

Naomi sits in her office for a while, contemplating what she wants to write about. She even prays to the Lord for a read-worthy article to enter her mind.

"Lord, I do not know what is going on with me. Are you speaking, and I am not listening? I need something, Lord. I will not keep pushing this. I know you will give me the right direction when it is time. In your precious name. Amen." Naomi closes her prayer.

Naomi continues through the week, and she decides to go to the studio she is renting out until she is able to buy her own outright. As she is going over dances for her girls, she thinks about the amazing times she had with her father.

It has been a few days since she has seen any of the guys. Ekon pops up on Naomi at the studio. Ekon is her humorous friend. He can keep you laughing even when you do not feel like laughing. Ekon owns his own Veterinary clinic and he truly loves animals. He will take in a stray, whatever it is, in a heartbeat.

"Yo, yo, yo Naomi, beomi, fe, fi, romi, Naooomi!" Ekon rhymes jokily.

They both laugh and give each other a huge hug.

"Man, E, you always playing. What's up today? I am surprised you got away from the clinic today." Naomi says.

"Well, I came by to check on one of the best Ladies I know. Also, I wanted to holla at you about something. You got time?" Ekon questions curiously.

"Yes, what going on? Oh, real quick, how's Paulie?" Naomi excitedly asks.

Paulie is the raccoon Ekon rescued outside in the backyard when he was trapped from eating the garbage and broke all his legs.

Ekon replies, "He is actually doing better. He stays at the clinic full time. You know Monica is not having a wild animal staying at the house. Barely can have a dog. "

"I can see you have really grown attached to him, so what is on your mind? Looks like it is something that is keeping you from resting." Naomi notices.

"Well, Monica told me that if I do not get my act together, she is gone, and I think she is for real this time." E nervously states.

"Well, is she wrong?" Naomi fires back.

Ekon shrugs and answers, "None whatsoever! Actually that is why I came by as well. You know I am a good dude, Naomi. My parents molded me to be a man. I had some wild teenage years, hell even in my early twenties, but I never did women wrong. I finally feel like I am in love, but I am hurting. Monica constantly belittles me and throws shade at my gift to help animals. She could care less if I go or come. Bottom line, it got to be another dude. I realize I can be so mean to her and act like I give other females attention, but that is truly because I know Monica does not care about me. I yearn for her attention and love, but instead, it is pushing us further apart."

"Wait, Ekon, I am so sorry you have been feeling like this, but I commend you for expressing your concerns. Have you tried to talk to Monica about what is on your heart?" Naomi questions.

As E is wiping away tears and folds his arms, he shakes his head continuously and replies. "No, no, I could not take this to her. She would devour my existence."

"Ekon, do you think this is healthy, being in a relationship you cannot even express yourself in? We can pray on it, that God gives you the words you need to express yourself to Mon. How does that sound?" Naomi asks while giving him a hug, wiping his tears.

Ekon nods his head and replies, "Yea, yea, we can do that."

"Oh Lord, my heavenly father, we come to you as humbly as we know how. First, I want to thank you for another day to be able to have life again. Lord, Ekon came to me to listen to his heart in confidence. Give his heart the courage to form the words in his mind to approach Monica. I ask that you give Monica the ears to receive it and the mind to digest it. We know relationships are not easy, but if we keep you as the beacon of our life, you will shine and guide us to the right path. Please order our footsteps today. In Jesus's name Amen." Naomi closes the prayer.

They both raise up their heads, hug, and praise God.

"Hallelujah, thank you, father!" Ekon exclaims.

"You know you can pray a mighty prayer. Thank you for showing your brother some love." Ekon continues to say.

"Anytime, bro, as long as I can breathe in air in my lungs, I will continue to pray for and with you. Now you need to get back to the clinic. You know they act like they cannot function without you!" Naomi laughs, jokily.

"Ha, you sholl right. Alright, Naomi, beomi, fe, fi, Naomi." He runs out as Naomi playfully swings at him.

"Alright now!" In Naomi's Angela Bassets voice and points.

Chapter 2
Faith Beyond Measure

Naomi remanences on her father's passing back in NOLA. Moved to STL to be with her mother at 13. Dance and God was her only outlet. Ballet is how Naomi cleanses her soul and frees her mind. It is a victorious escape, going to Cathedral (Mount Sinai), where she is close with the current Bishop, who is the Bishop's uncle and mentor.

"Daddy, daddy. I want my father! No, get off of me, I said get off of me now. I will not leave here without my daddy." Young Naomi screams in anguish.

"Come on here gal, yo daddy will catch up with you later. If we leave you here, you sho gone die." The elderly neighbor pleaded with Naomi.

Naomi kicked and screamed while the neighbor and her husband got her on the rescue raft.

She heard from several other New Orleanians that the workers down at the oil rig on the river fought to get to safety, but none of them survived. Naomi refused to accept the news.

One glad morning when this life is over, I'll fly away. Oh glory. When I die, hallelujah by and by. I'll fly away. Naomi overhears the choir singing from outside the cathedral.

"Bishop is going to throw down preaching the word today. And this song resonates in my soul. I missed the first few minutes of devotion so I know he is going to be on my head." Naomi softly thinks to herself.

As she walks into the church, she drops her keys and purse. She picks up her Bible first because she has a belief of not mishandling the word of God. As she bends over again to get her keys this time, a clean-cut, well-dressed, heavenly-smelling gentleman picks them up for her.

Naomi thinks to herself, "Lord, if this is a wolf in sheep's clothing, just say that!" Naomi laughs to herself.

"Was there something amusing?" The gentlemen curiously questions.

"Oh no, no, no. I just had a thought about something when I went to pick up my keys. I do appreciate it. Well, we better get in the church, I am sure they are introducing visitors by now." Naomi advises.

"You are right. Well, I will see you around sometime." The gentleman smiles and walks ahead of Naomi.

Naomi finds her seat close to the front and Bishop gives her a look for walking in late. Naomi waves hello, as she feels her gut sink. Bishop was just allowing the announcer to welcome the visitors. She excitedly waits for the unknown visitor to stand.

"We would like to welcome all that have been led to congregate with us here at Mount Sinai. We would love to hear from any visitors today. If you are visiting with Mount Sinai, please stand. Don't be shy." The announcer greets.

"Hello everyone, First I would like to give the glory to my Heavenly Father who is the head of my life. Today I am here to visit my uncle." The gentleman holds his hand out toward the front of the cathedral.

Naomi looks around to determine who this mystery man's uncle is. He continues to speak.

"My uncle, Bishop Rutherford was the man to step in and be a male figure to me when my father could not be. He led me down the right path and has taught me the word of God. He has taught me the importance of not just reading the word but living the word. I am here to stay for a while, so I do not know if that would classify me as a visitor or not. I am Bishop Cleveland and I am the Bishop in training." He states firmly.

The entire congregation stands and claps. They welcome him with open arms. The announcer closes her visitor welcome, "We welcome you once, we welcome you twice, we welcome you in the name of Jesus Christ. Now I will turn it over to the hands of Bishop Rutherford." Bishop Rutherford steps to the pulpit and speaks more about Bishop and how he is blessed to have him in the house of the Lord. To mold him into the Bishop that the world needs.

Naomi sits there and she is amazed. She has a feeling that she has not felt ever. She continues to listen to Bishop's Chosen sermon and it resonates with her soul. Once Bishop finishes the sermon, and it is now called to discipleship, he asks for his nephew Bishop to lead the cathedral in prayer.

Bishop prays and it is a mighty prayer. The congregation is at their feet praising God for the words he prayed. As the congregation is exiting the cathedral and mingling with one another, Bishop calls Naomi over.

"Naomi, darling, come here for just a moment. I know you have to get over to the studio. This will not take long. I want to introduce you to my nephew Bishop Cleveland, this is basically my son." Bishop chuckles and claps Bishop on the back.

"Yes, we met Bishop. Bishop was kind enough to pick up my keys when I dropped them trying to rush in this morning." She bashfully smiles.

"Yeah uncle, she graced my presence on this fine Sunday morning. Well, I will not hold you. Uncle said you have somewhere to be." Bishop confirms.

Both walk towards her vehicle.

"I do. I am a dance instructor for little girls here in the community. Well, that is until I get my studio open, and I will be instructing them from my own space." Naomi continues.

"That sounds amazing. I would love to hear more." Bishop states.

"You just may. We shall see Mr. Bishop Cleveland. By the way, kind of funny that your name is Bishop and you are in training to become a Bishop. Meant to be, I guess." Naomi slightly laughs, getting into her SUV.

"That it is." Bishop says as he holds his hand up.

Naomi can see Bishop's hand in her rearview mirror. She pulls up to the studio she is currently renting for her girls. This is her third home. Her girls are her life, and dance is her baby.

"Alright, ladies. Ms. Naomi has arrived. Thank you, thank you." She playfully dances into the building as the girls run up to her.

"You are late, Ms. Naomi." Little Ms. Shyann says demandingly.

"I know, ladies, today has been a late start for me. I do apologize. What have I taught you all?" She questions.

"If you are early, you are simply on time. If you are on time, you are late. Might as well back up and get the heck out of there!" All the girls loudly reply.

"Alright now, baby!" Naomi says in her NOLA voice.

The girls and Naomi line up in front of the mirror. They get into position one to begin their ballet routine. Once they finish their ballet routines, they wrap up with a praise and worship dance. Naomi believes in giving all praise to God. Then, ending in prayer.

"Oh Lord, my heavenly father. First, we want to thank you for allowing us to come together another time and enjoy another amazing time. We expressed ourselves in dance and exalted your name. Forgive me for being late to Sundays service. Forgive me for being late to dance practice. May this week be filled with joy, success, and many, blessings. In your most holy name, let us all say." Naomi closes.

All the girls reply, "Amen!"

As Naomi lines her girls up for rehearsal, she is elated by their progress and how much they love the Lord. She could not ask for anything greater. The girls wrap up and give Naomi hugs as their parents pick them up.

One of her students walk over to her and begins to converse with her.

"Miss Naomi, you know sometimes I see you go into a daze, and it seems something deep is on your mind. My mama always tells me to take it to the Lord and lay it at his feet. Let the Lord fight your battle, okay!" Little Roxi runs off to her mother.

Naomi sits on the dance floor and stares off into the large studio mirrors. As the music continues to play, she remanences about when she was robbed of her childhood.

"Mama, Mama! Are you ready? You have to get me to school by 9:15 AM. Mr. Johnson said I could not be late again or they would call Child Protective Services. I know you do not want to lose me again to the system. Mama!" Naomi yells out.

"Huh." Oleatha mutters.

Oleatha was laid out on the floor, high out of her mind. She would not let Naomi's father take her in. Of course, there was shame for losing Naomi before.

Naomi's mother never raised up. She had to walk to school, knowing this would be the last time she saw her mother. Naomi was tired of covering and protecting her mother. There was an abundance of hope she had in her mother. Hope that one day she would wake up and get clean. CPS was already waiting at the school. Although Naomi was young, CPS listened to her strong voice.

"I would feel most comfortable and in great hands with my father. My mother did not want me to be with him, but I wanted to live with my father. He is a great man. My father is a loving man." Naomi explains.

The CPS social worker nodded her head and guided Naomi to the CPS car. It was a process, but her father pushed through to get custody of Naomi. Naomi had to stay in a group home for six months before she could depart with her father.

While in the group home, the experience was not as bad as she imagined it would be. There were many shattered children, but why wouldn't they be? Given the situations, they have all been through.

Naomi would then dance around in front of the bay windows, and all of the children and group workers would admire her performance. Once she tired herself out, she would then sit in the bay window and write. She would always notice a boy around the same age as her that would stare at her. Naomi never got weird vibes from him staring. That did not frighten her one bit. One day Naomi decided to invite him to sit in the bay window with her and write. She simply patted the seat and reached her arm out with the notebook and pen. The boy would not talk. He would communicate with her through pen and paper.

They would laugh and play silent games, all on paper. Until one day, he decided to speak. The silence was broken.

"You know, many people do not get why I am different. Why I am quiet and reserved. I have always loved to be around the women in my life. I loved how they nurtured us children and took extra time to understand our feelings. I scared my mother for a while, being young and so different. She thought I was going to become what society was pushing out there. She eventually loved me for me. She did not love me enough to keep her filthy brother away from me." The boy snarled.

"Your Uncle?" Naomi gasps.

"Her brother." The boy opposes.

Naomi grabs his hand as he continues to explain his story.

"An uncle would never commit such heinous crimes. He would always whisper to me, 'I will show you what a man is all about, a grown man.' He did not give me a chance to be a child. He robbed me of my innocence. That man led me to manhood before my time. My mother did not love me. I do not think I will ever accept a woman's love." The boy cries.

Naomi wipes his eyes and just holds him.

"It is alright. My childhood got tarnished too. We will overcome." Naomi reassures.

"So you know my life story? What is your name anyway?" The boy asks Naomi.

"Well, I thought you would never ask. I am Naomi Cleveland. And yours?" She questions the boy.

"My name is Malachi Pope. Nice to meet you, Naomi!" Malachi laughs excitedly.

From that day forth, Naomi and Malachi were inseparable.

Naomi's father finally received custody of her. Sadly, she had to leave Malachi.

"We will have to keep in touch, Malachi. We have been together for months, and neither of our birthdays have passed. When is your birthday?" Naomi questions.

"September 11, 1990." Malachi says proudly.

"Stop playing. That is my exact birthday!" Naomi laughs out.

"That is why we click so well. Nothing like a Virgo baby." Malachi proclaimed.

"You know what, you my twin flame. We connected forever. Even while I am hundreds of miles away." Naomi says.

"Fo' sho.' Guess you gone have to call me Flame. I am hotter than hot tamale." Flame says conceitedly.

"There we have it, my Flame." Naomi agrees.

Naomi leaves with her father and prepares for the long road trip ahead of them to New Orleans. Flame and Naomi would talk on the phone on a daily basis after school. During the summers, Naomi's father would get permission to take Flame for a few weeks. Naomi helped Flame to be comfortable with himself. To trust men again and know that women loved him. Naomi would pray with him. Some nights they would sit on the phone and just write about how they felt.

"Flame, you are awfully quiet tonight. Is there something on your mind?" Naomi asks curiously.

"I truly have been healing from my past trauma and I have you and the Lord to thank for this. It is just that." Flame pauses.

"It is okay Flame. You know your words are safe with me." Naomi reassures.

"There was this one night her brother played too drunk to drive home. Of course, my mama did not play about drinking and driving, so he preyed on that. Soon as my mama was asleep, I heard my door creak open. I could smell the Martell coming out of his pores. Too cheap to buy Courvoisier, hell Hennessy, my mother would always say. That night I did not care how cheap he was. I just did not want him to molest me again. He laid with me and cuddled with me as if I was his woman. He whispered in my ear, 'only men can give it to you like this baby.' I stabbed him that night. I never told anyone how I ended up in the foster home. My mother took the rap. So now she is doing a bid for me. For my sins. Of course, I did not have anyone to take me in, so the state had to." Flame breaks down.

Naomi sat in silence for a while to let Flame release his pain and to absorb what he had just told her.

Chapter 3
Typical Where

Bishop notices that Naomi has her dance attire hanging out of her dance bag and he approaches her as she is walking into the Cathedral.

"Bonjour, Madam Naomi." Bishop speaks in his fluent French accent.

"Bonjour Monsieur Bishop." Naomi speaks in her broken French accent.

"So you know how to speak French"? Bishop questions with a puzzled look.

"Just a bit, only took French my freshman year and I could not make it the last three years." She laughs.

"Good to see you again." Bishop happily states.

"Likewise." Naomi agrees.

"So, what are you doing later today? I mean, I know you were saying you wanted to hear more about my studio and all, so I figured we could stop by the coffee shop after service. I do not have class until 3 today," Naomi curiously asks.

"That will be perfect. I will meet you here after service." Bishop smiles and walks tall with his hands in his straight-legged dress pants into the Cathedral. Naomi just stands there and watches how he struts into the building.

After service concludes and Bishop completes his final words with his Uncle Bishop Rutherford, he walks over to Naomi's SUV.

"So shall we head to the coffee shop? I know you have a busy day ahead of you?" Bishop questions.

"It ain't that busy, but yes, of course, let's get going. You want to trail behind me? Keep up now. I do not go slow." Naomi jokes.

She sits back in her seat and makes sure her seatbelt is secure, and her lipstick is intact. Bishop turns around, and he can see her getting herself together in her left side mirror. As he walks to his vehicle, he smiles with beatitude.

Bishop and Naomi arrive at Jed Muddy Uptown Dining Cafe downtown Saint Louis. Bishop walks to Naomi's SUV and opens the door for her.

He holds out his hand, "Madamoiselle." Then he slightly bows.

Naomi blushes with gleam. She thinks to herself how this man is a whole gentleman. There has to be a catch, although she does not want to think that way. Even good men have some slick ways. Well, that is what her mother told her growing up.

As they walk into the coffee shop, they admire all the historical paintings and pictures of Saint Louis. There are people there enjoying books, conducting business meets, and meeting for friendly gatherings. The two of them sit down in a secluded section. For a moment, they look over the beverage menu to decide what they want to order.

Naomi looks up at Bishop and a breeze blows past her face. She goes into a daze. She remembers the one time that her father was unpleasant in her eyes.

Naomi and her father would read different types of books to explore the world. They would enjoy the ends and outs of the life that her father created for them. It was Naomi and Pa against the world.

"Is everything alright? We do not have to order anything if you are not feeling this spot." Bishop questions with curiosity.

Naomi can see his lips moving, but she is not completely back to reality. Bishop touches her hand and she pulls herself back to reality.

"I'm, I'm alright. I just need to go to the ladies' room for a moment." Naomi says with hesitation.

Naomi walks to the restroom, where she stands in front of the sink. She places her hands on the counter and rocks back and forth. Then looks up to the mirror. The thoughts that she has about her father are making her feel uneasy, although she wants to enjoy this moment getting to know Bishop. She gets herself together, pats her face, and smooths her dress down. As she is walking to the table, she sees Bishop's Uncle in the window of the small cafe. Seeing Bishop Rutherford standing in the window and she realizes, "This is where it happened."

Her father had backdoor passes. No one entered in front unless there were important elected officials like President Joe Biden or Vice President Kamala Harris and her second man in charge. As a child, she played the flute to hear the gentleness of the tone in the atmosphere. Her father brought her the things she needed to be outstanding in this field of music. He made sure she was well taken care of. Until one day, her mother rushed through the cafe doors. The important people's status went out the window. She pranced up to my father and slapped fire from him. He held his composure. She yelled at him for taking me to the cafe with all those rich white folk. Her mother felt second to her father's success, although he tried to make her a priority. Drugs were

Naomi's mother's priority. But the way the system is set up, mothers can go to court and throw all types of lies to keep their child. Her father stopped fighting. He let Naomi go with Oletha. From time to time, Oletha would let Naomi go with her father. That was only when she got tired of being a mother. The bond between Naomi and her father did not diminish. In fact it flourished.

Naomi's father would talk to her all night about her plans and vision to be successful. She wondered who could ask for a better father.

Until one day, Naomi's father was unpleasant to her. They went to the Cafe when he came to town. As they were walking in, Naomi noticed her father was not walking with her anymore. He stopped, laid his eyes on this gray and green-eyed, straight pepper and salt-haired Australian woman. Her perfume smelled expensive. Smelt like something that came out of a garden; purple lilies maybe.

At the time, Naomi did not know what her father was doing or who this woman would become. Things went left quickly. Her father would pick Naomi up and Amelia would be shotgun, smoking a long Virginia Slim. Surprisingly, she loved fishing and her Pa's pockets. Amelia caught a large catfish. Her father told Naomi to take the fish off the hook for Amelia. Of course, she did not want to get those soft, moisturized hands dirty. Naomi took the fish that Amelia caught and put it in a 1967 Ford Falcon XR GT like a V8 Mustang Sedan. Naomi began to have a strong dislike for this woman. Pa and Amelia planned a trip to Australia. Of course, they paid for the entire trip. Amelia would beg to go to Coogee Beach within Sydney, Australia and her father would honor her wish. Naomi asked if she could accompany Amelia and her father later to kayak, snorkel, scuba diving, stand-up paddle or something. They were too into each other to hear her wishes.

Naomi loved bathing in the Bondi Iceberg when she was left alone. It is an oceanfront famous in Sydney.

Bishop Rutherford finally makes his way over to the table.

"If I would of known you two were coming to the café I, I would have asked for a lift." He humorously laughs.

"Unc, I believe something is going on with Naomi. She has been in this trance for some time now. I ordered us both a frappe." Bishop pauses.

" Let me talk with her for a moment. You mind going to order a coffee, black for an old man?" Bishop Rutherford reassures.

Bishop walks over to the ordering line and he glances over to the table with genuine concern.

"Sis Naomi, are you reflecting on things. Naomi, honey, you are alright. Is there some things that triggered this spell?" Bishop Rutherford examines.

"Yesss, my father was so kind and loving. He let the wrong woman into his life. He loved this woman more than me. I forgave him, Bishop. I adored my father and he let me down like my mother let me down." Naomi softly cries.

Bishop is still briefly glancing to make sure Naomi is alright.

Bishop Rutherford begins to intercede on Naomi's behalf. He prays over her mind that she can get past the hurt and pain from both of her parents.

Bishop walks over to the table with his uncle's black coffee.

"Black as tar, just how you prefer." Bishop jokes.

"Thanks, son. Well, I will be on my way. Naomi is just fine. We just needed to have a storytime.

"I am glad to see you alright, Naomi. You had me worried there." Bishop confesses.

"I apologize, at times, I have these moments. Moments from my past that I am healing from. Certain things can trigger those thoughts. The main reason people should not suppress their feelings." Naomi explains.

"I hate that we did not get to talk and enjoy these delicious frappes together, but I have to get over to the studio. Please forgive me." Naomi pleas.

"One thing you will have to do is stop apologizing for everything. You are fine. We all need to take time and take care of our mental health and I know duty calls. Get to your girls. We will have another time." Bishop promises.

Bishop offers to pay, but Naomi wants to pay her own tab. Not to make Bishop feel less of a man but to express that she can hold her own and not use him for his money.

"Thank you for understanding. I will see you soon, Monsieur Bishop." Naomi states.

Bishop confirms, "Until we meet again, Madame Naomi."

Naomi goes to the studio and begins the class with prayer. The girls tell all their exciting stories from the week and they begin dance. She explains to the girls that soon, she will need to teach them a routine for the grand opening of her own studio.

Once Naomi leaves the studio, she sits in her SUV and thinks about her reflections from earlier but not for too long. She prayed with Bishop Rutherford, let go, and let God.

Naomi drives home from a long work week and a fulfilling word from God. She sends a group chat to the fellas. She has big news for them and an even enormous question to ask them. Drinks and a dinner prepared by her would be perfect.

Naomi sits on her daybed in her bay window and pulls out her iPhone.

Begins to text in the group chat.

"Y'all know what time it is!!

I'm hoping all y'all are free tomorrow night at 7.

I have some exciting news that I want to share.

So be there or be square!" With celebratory emojis.

Ekon replies back immediately,

"I know the Virgin Mary only walked the Earth once!" He sends laughing emojis.

Naomi does not reply. She knows Ekon is always stirring up something, and she does not want to entertain that.

Hunter has joined the chat with crying laughing emoji's.

"Idiota." Javier replies.

The conversation goes on until everyone arrives the next day at Naomi's loft.

Naomi finishes making dinner. They all love her zesty-baked Salmon, rice pilaf, and grilled vegetables. Naomi can hear the guys on the elevator. She has a tray of champagne glasses and she waits at the elevator gate. The gate slides up.

"Alright, where the party at!" Ekon shouts out.

"Fellas, let us leave that right here. Turn that arguing off, and Ekon, just turn down." Naomi demands.

Hunter kisses Naomi on the hand, "Howdy darling."

Naomi smiles, "Hey Hunt."

She turns back to Javier and Enrique. As usual, Flame is late.

Twenty minutes into dinner, the elevator goes down to the ground floor. The elevator rises back to her floor. Flame speeds off of the elevator with Peony's, which are her favorite. He goes to hug Naomi and she is angry.

"No Flame, you cannot Waltz in here looking like Rico Suave and can woo me with some flowers. Save that for your lil tenders!" Naomi goes off.

All the guys are looking down, and at the sametime they glance their eyes up at Naomi and Flame. Naomi begins to laugh with the guys.

"Nah, bro. Naomi, not going to keep putting up with your tardiness." E points out.

"Tardiness. What is this school? Boy, bye! See, what you not gone do is tell me what she gone do. Naomi is her own woman." Flames fires back.

Flame and E are now going at it. Hunter is just sitting at the end of the table, looking out the window. Javier is silently laughing, shaking his head.

Hunter pulls himself from the window as he thinks about Elizabeth. He stops the guys again.

"Naomi called all of us here for some news. Can y'all chill for once?" Hunter questions.

Flame and Ekon pause on their debate.

"Okay, Pops. You always want to be somebody's father." Flames says as he pours himself more champagne.

E stands next to Naomi with serious curiosity and puts his jokes to the side.

"Not trying to rush Naomi, but the sitter said she cannot watch Nubia all night for me. Something about this being her date night." Hunter discloses.

"Of course, I will make this quick as possible. You have to get home to our princess. So as you all know, I plan on leaving the studio early next year here in Saint Louis. I been reading out to investors abroad. That being said, I will be going to Australia to discuss my business and I can bring others along to demonstrate other businesses in the United States." Naomi shouts excitedly.

All the guys applaud and rejoice with Naomi.

"Look at God, Bad Bih going abroad." Flame celebrates.

"Did you just curse and use God in the same sentence?" E questions.

"He did." Hunter agrees.

"Let me move over. I know God has been waiting to strike you." Ekon states shakily.

"See, idiota." Javier laughs.

"But anyway, Naomi, you know your brothers are beyond elated for this opportunity. God is good." E states as he raises his champagne glass to the air.

The guys and Naomi also raise their glasses and salute.

"Naomi, you are truly a gift to this world. Congratulations." Hunter celebrates.

"Felcitaciones mi amor." Javier speaks.

The guys shout, "Speak English!" Then everyone begins to laugh.

"Now this trip, I need my boys to come with me. Whatever donations you receive, put it towards your business needs." Naomi generously offers.

"Naomi, we are for sure going to attend the event. Whatever we are blessed with from this event, it is yours. Vanessa Butterfly is going to take over the map!" Ekon shouts out.

"Ahhh!" Naomi shouts back.

Everyone continues to celebrate for the duration of the night.

Naomi notices that Enrique was not very talkative. He congratulated her new opportunity and agreed to go on the trip but something was off. It has been a while since she has seen Rique and has been taking clients in all fifty states.

"Hey." Naomi says with a mellow tone as she bumps her shoulder against his.

"Hey. You ready for this big trip? I know I am. I have been all over, but Australia is the first." Rique gently laughs.

Naomi laughs with him and says, "Well, I have been a few times but not as pleasant. I will be with my brothers, so we are bound to have a great time. Maybe we can count how many times people will think I am dating all of y'all."

"Yeah, I am ready to hear your next comeback. You are such a firecracker. You have calmed down since college, though." Enrique mentions.

"So enough about me and this trip. What has been going on with you? I have not seen you in a while and it seems like we have not had a talk. FaceTime does no justice." Says Naomi.

"Naomi, do you think I am crazy? Sometimes I just cannot get out of bed. I cannot eat. All I want to do is sleep the day away. I feel guilty being here and the woman in the next car over lost her life so gruesomely. I should have lost my life. I did not give reverence to God the way I should have. That woman was a grandmother. She went to your church. She was a mother of the church. She cooked breakfast for the Bishop every Sunday. I do not deserve to be here." Enrique whispers to Naomi.

Naomi walks around to Enrique's face. She hugs him for a moment and replies.

"Do you think any of us deserve to be here? We sin daily and are so ungrateful to the sacrifice that Jesus laid his life on the cross for our sins. We all fall short of God's glory. Romans 3:10 states, 'There is none righteous, no, not one.' Therefore none of us are exempt from being in God's wrath. God gives us chance after chance to make things right. To truly ask for forgiveness. We all fall in the category of sinner and unworthy. But HE sees your worth, so continue to live in your purpose and do not let this feeling consume you. You are a great man Rique. You know I ride with you like two flats on a 'Lac." Naomi jokes.

"Naomi, what we gone do without you homie. You gone continue to roll with us and we gone ride for you. Thank you for opening my eyes to the Lord and what he has done for me. I will continue to walk in his glory." Enrique gives praises to God.

Hunter grabs his car keys and tells the fellow goodbye. He gives Naomi a hug and congratulates her once more before he heads out. He stayed longer than he anticipated. The sitter will have lots to say but everyone knows she loves Nubia and would stop the world for her.

Naomi does her final cleaning of the loft. Takes an extended bubble bath in her bowl tub and thinks about the night. She sits in her bay window for a moment and watches the rain hit the windowpane. Then walks over to her California king-size bed. She gets on her knees, reads her favorite passage, Ecclesiastes 3:1-8, and prays.

"Oh Lord, my heavenly father. First, I want to ask you to forgive me for all my sins. Things I knowingly and unknowingly done. The things I intentionally and unintentionally did. I ask you to forgive any anger I have in my heart. I thank you for another beautiful day to get things right. I thank you for allowing me to see my brothers one more time and get their support in my next chapter. I pray that you can lead and guide me to the right path. I pray to get closer to you and live in my purpose. Cover my brothers with their daily battles. Lord, I ask you to cover my girls as they attend school. Lord, I ask that my relationship with my mother gets stronger. You know it has been a rocky relationship all my life; she is all I have left on this earth and I want a bond with her. I want her to see me get married. I want her to approve of my future husband. I want her to love on her grandchildren. And before I let you go Lord, I do not know where this friendship is going with Bishop but I have to say, I like him. I do not want to lose sight of you though, Lord. If this is something that fits in to what you have for me, lead it, Lord. In the mighty name of Jesus. Amen!

After church, it became a thing for Naomi and Bishop to meet up after church at the cafe. The atmosphere was always casual, never pressured. The friendship is different than what she has with Enrique, Javier, Flame, Ekon, and Hunter. They are her brothers. Her brothers in Christ. The friendship she is receiving from Bishop was different than her father's. He was her Pa, counselor, and best friend. He taught her how men operate. He guided her, molded her for the world. The friendship with Bishop felt spiritual. They prayed together, deep prayers at that. The prayers were for each other's good, for their salvation. The bond was becoming platonic. There was chemistry but neither of them pursued each other sexually. This was more than a friend zone. This was bigger than lust. The smile they put on each other's face was refreshing. Naomi felt it would be beneficial to invite Bishop along to the trip. She could learn more about him being a Bishop; maybe a new article for her. More about his life. Her brothers could get a feel for him. Then just maybe, she could take him home to mama.

The first trip to Australia for the event, Naomi asks Bishop to accompany her. Both Naomi and Bishop demonstrate to each other that neither are the typical male and female.

Why go to Australia? Need investors to operate new businesses in Sydney.

Bishop's mother and father lived in the suburbs of Saint Louis, Ballwin to be exact. He had both of his parents for the majority of his childhood. Until one day, his father got up and left him and his mother high and dry. He never heard from his father again.

Bishop got a job at a Christian bookstore to support his mother. His uncle would visit every week to encourage his mother through bible study and prayer. Bishop Rutherford also paid for Bishop to get through seminary school.

Chapter 4
Abroad Awaits (Life Skills)

Naomi, Bishop and the fellas arrive in Adelaide, Australia. Naomi always wanted to visit Australia. The last time she was there, it felt as if she was there all alone. This time will have a meaning and purpose. In addition, Naomi was there with those she cared for the most. She loves the Sydney Opera House from the pictures, of course. How crisp the air looks? The water radiantly blue. The culture and accents. Naomi is finally living the reality she dreamt of once again. Who would fathom such an experience?

"Thank you, Lord!" Naomi exclaims.

"Yes, Praise him, honey!" Flame agrees.

"Well, I am beat. I already know this time difference is going to kill me. I will see y'all at dinner." Enrique states.

"Same here." Ekon agrees and continues to say, "Mon probably celebrating my absence; I will call her to confirm. Ekon jokes sadly walks away.

"E, I am positive she misses you. Absence makes the heart grow fonder." Naomi quotes.

"And it makes the heart grow fondler!!" Enrique cracks up in laughter.

"See, Naomi, I do not even know why you invited him. Who wants to know how to cut their grass? Like we don't already know how to do that!" E states aggressively.

"Maybe if you did know how, your wife wouldn't be." Enrique continues.

"Woah, woah, woah. Hold on fellas." Bishop interjects.

"Exactly. Wow, we all know how I feel about us being on the same page. You two better not start. Let us show love on this trip and represent the Lou right. We will meet you guys at 7. Okay?" Naomi proceeds.

"Yeah, okay." The guys agree and walk off.

A phone begins to ring. Bishop and Naomi both check their phones due to their ringtones being the same.

"Not mine, must be yours." Bishop laughs.

The phone stops ringing and Bishop and Naomi begin to walk to the elevators. The phone starts to ring again. Naomi places her rolling luggage by the elevator and she scrabbles through her cross-body Aldo purse. Naomi finally finds her phone underneath all her essentials. She looks at her phone and her mother Oletha has called her twenty times.

"Now my mother knows the flight time was twenty hours. Why did she have to blow me up like this? As if we were the missing passengers on flight 828." Naomi rambles on.

"Hold on now, she just worried, I am sure. Look at the bright side. You were telling me how she abandoned you when you needed you most. Now she is just making up for lost time and trying to be the best mother she can. Try not to take it the wrong way. She loves you, Naomi." Bishop explains.

Bishop and Naomi walk to their separate rooms that are on the same floor. The rooms are down the hall from each other and Naomi's room is up first.

"I really cannot believe E and Riq. They have always fought like brothers. Riq knows exactly how to get under E's skin. I do not know what they would do without me." Naomi knowingly questions.

"You know, I bet they ask themselves the same thing. I bet even God is shaking his head. But got to love these guys." Bishop states.

Naomi inputs her room card into the reader and cracks the door open.

"Here we are, 777. Now, how you get this room? You got a winning number. Many would say you are lucky." Bishop chuckles.

"Fun fact, did you know the number seven is a sign of completion?" Naomi questions.

"Actually, I remember my uncle preaching about that as a child. It is complete, my queen." Bishop gleams.

"Is that so?" Naomi proceeds to enter her room.

"See you later, Mr. Cleveland." Naomi bashfully murmured.

"Until then, Ms. Russell." Reassured Bishop. He nods and walks down the hall to his room.

Naomi walks into her room and places her luggage next to the closet door. Then goes to the large king-size bed and sits on the edge. She thinks about the last words Bishop said. She whispers, "My Queen." Then she shakes her head.

"Girl, do not think too hard about that. That is what all the guys say now. I am sure that does not mean anything." She assures herself.

Naomi then pulls out her phone to call her mother back; she really does not want her to worry about them. As she dials her mother's number, she looks out the window at Australia's beauty.

Oletha answers, "Hello! I called you too many times, baby. Got me worried. I was gone get on one of those planes and find you and them boys. I thought maybe that man done kidnapped y'all." Oletha chatters on.

"What man, mama? Bishop?" Naomi questions.

"Yes! These people crazy now a days. I thought I was going to have to get on that plane and show y'all I am from the show me state. Do not try, Oletha!" She replies.

Naomi laughs. "Mama, you are so silly. You sat there and thought about all this. But did not think about how long the flight is and how we had to get the luggage, and get settled at the resort?" Naomi questions.

"Well, that is true, but you know I never flew on a plane before. Barely ever left Saint Louis. But thank God, I left Saint Louis to visit with your father to NOLA. I would not have had you, baby." Oleatha says proudly.

"Alright now, mama, I have to meet the fellas and our kidnapper downstairs. So I will call you when I get back to the room. It will probably be late. There is a time difference so remember that, mama." Naomi laughs.

Her mother begins to laugh also. "Okay baby, enjoy yourself. I am at ease now. I love you."

"Love you too, Mama. Talk to you later." Naomi agrees.

Naomi heads to the massive bathroom. She places all her makeup, skincare products, hair products, and personal hygiene products on the counter. She turns the shower on and feels the perfect temperature. Naomi also turns on her smooth jazz. She enters the shower and vibes to the jazz. Thoughts begin to fill her mind about the beautiful dinner tonight and what the trip will entail. Maybe she will get a dance in with Bishop. That is if he asks, of course. When she gets out of the shower, she lathers her body in baby oil so that the fragrance can stick to her body. She washes her face with Fenty Skin by Rihanna. Then she puts on her Mac makeup. Now that she is all dolled up and ready to step on necks, she walks down the hall. Several women compliment her style. That was different for Naomi because compliments are rare in Saint Louis. The acknowledgement felt good and refreshing.

Everyone meets up in the dining area promptly to have dinner together. Naomi proceeds down the stairs with an elegant satin gown on. Flame is at the bottom of the staircase and he holds his hand out to assist her off the last step. Bishop is in awe of Naomi's beauty. All of the guys proceed to walk behind her into the dining room. Women and men look puzzled and confused as to why a group of men was accompanying her. She holds her head high and walks proudly to the table.

"Allow me." Bishop gladly demands as he pulls out Naomi's chair.

"You may." Naomi giggles.

Flame lets go of Naomi so that she can sit at the table. Bishop helps her scoot up to the table.

"Naomi wanna walk in as showstopper? Alright now. Do not make me call mama." Enrique jokes.

"Stop it, Riq, please do not call her. You know I always have to come presentable. One thing my mama taught me is to make sure you leave out presentable; you do not know who you may meet." Naomi gives a quick lesson.

" Speak it, Naomi beomi." Ekon starts to rhyme.

"Naw, do not start that here." Naomi stops E.

Bishop looks around the table and embraces the love that they all share. Everyone continues to converse and laugh. Several women walk up to the table, asking to dance with the fellas. One woman, in particular, asked Bishop to escort her to the dance floor.

Bishop gave an uninterested look and kindly replied, "no thank you, love; I would ask one of these fine gentlemen at the table. Except for him, he is married." Bishop points to Ekon.

She pushes up on Bishop forcing him to take her to the floor. Bishop gives in and states, "One dance and then I will have to let you go."

"We will see about that." The woman winks a Bishop.

Bishop looks at Naomi and she looks away. Naomi looks as if it did not phase her, truly it did.

"I see that look, sis." Enrique points out.

"What look, Rique, do not play with me." Naomi fired back.

"Don't you play with me? You think we do not see the blushing and the he-ha-ha between y'all?" Rique continues.

"Oh really, so y'all just sitting around talking about us? Well, there is no us. He is a good friend like y'all are. That is ALL!" Naomi turns and looks at the dance floor.

"Now you know dang on well, that is not a good friend. I see you glow and how he makes you smile. You better stop playing oblivious and non-chalant before Miss thang over there swoops him up. She looks like she will do it too." Enrique laughs.

Naomi laughs with Enrique because she knows what he is saying is the truth.

"You just might be on to something. So while y'all talking about me, let us talk about how you always starting stuff with E. You got to stop, especially with the Monica jokes. He is really going through with her right now. I will not go into details because he confided in me. But it has to end, Rique. Whatever beef y'all got with each other has got to stop too." Naomi lectures.

"Beef. Naomi, you know what beef I have with him. He was my best friend. Mine. Then he decides to step to my sister. What happened to bro code? We do not mess with our best friends' sisters. Monica is my little sister. The way he treats her upsets me and I cannot do anything because it is their business." Enrique aggressively rambles.

"You are exactly right, that is their business and there are things we may not fully understand. Just know Ekon loves Monica and he would not hurt her." Naomi assures.

Flame, Hunter, and Javier walk up to the table after having two plates each from the buffet.

"Dang, did we interrupt anything? Why is Rique's vein popping out of his neck?" Flame begins to laugh.

"Loco." Javier whispers as he gestures coo-coo to his ear.

"Y'all don't start. We were just having a deep conversation. I hear y'all were talking about me. So what's up? Naomi jokes.

"Naomi cannot hold water." Enrique states as he backs from the table and goes over to the buffet line to get food.

"Well." Naomi folds her arms.

Bishop walks fast back to the table. "I thought I was never going to get away. One of you guys are up next."

"I will go." Javier replies in English.

Javier proceeds to walk over to Miss Thang. She grabs him up and they begin to dance.

"Since when does he speak English? Something must be in the water. We probably will not be seeing Javier anymore tonight." Hunter jokes.

"We more than likely won't. Looks like he is where he wants to be. So since we have the majority of everyone at the table, let's talk about the event. I will catch Javier up in the morning." Naomi replies.

Naomi and the fellas go over the details for the event. They all celebrate and cheer each other on. Bishop and Naomi continue to stare at each other from across the round table. Everyone says their final good night and head to their rooms. Javier shared a room with Enrique and did not return until sunrise.

As the morning approaches, Naomi gets dressed and walks down the hall to Enrique and Javier's room. She knocks on the door and Enrique is ready to go. Javier is still knocked out across one of the queen-sized beds.

"Javi! Javier! Wake your butt up. Since when you staying out all night with random women." Naomi begins to laugh.

Rique laughs with her.

Javier replies…they go over the details.

Everyone gets off the plane, talking on and on about the trip. The guys continue to walk ahead. Naomi and Bishop stop to talk for a moment.

"Well, we are back to reality. So will you be gracing me with your presence sometime soon?" Bishop curiously asks.

"That depends. You have time to wait?" Naomi questions.

"I have all the time in the world. I want to get to know more of you." Bishop states.

"Alright then, sounds like we have a plan. I have several articles to submit. Of course, the article about your Bishop in training. Thank you again, by the way." Naomi thanks Bishop.

"Of course, I want the world to know about how there is great things coming in the catholic community. Hopefully, some changes will be made." Bishop ponders.

A FEW WEEKS GO BY…

Bishop and Naomi meet up a few times for occasional dates, several dates now to be exact.

The Best Part of Her

Chapter 5
She Works Hard

Bishop delivers a powerful sermon. Naomi Realizes that Bishop is the man for her. The guys notice that Naomi is not doing well and has a meeting with Bishop. Her mother tells Naomi she will need to slow down. Hire someone to teach the girls and take medical leave at work. Also need to put in for FMLA (family medical leave of absence). Naomi opposes until she cannot get out of bed one morning and reconsiders.

The sermon for this morning is Chosen: Time to Stand Out. The passage is coming from Ephesians 6:1." Bishop Cleveland asked Bishop to proceed with reading the scripture to the congregation. In unison the congregation shouted, "God bless the readers, the hearers, and the doers of his most holy word! Amen!" Everyone sat down across the congregation and listened to Bishop Cleveland deliver the word of God.

When you are chosen you can't do the things you used to do, which is of the world—staying out partying. ME, I did that! Eating any and everything is just messing up your health and body. ME! Watching and partaking in provocative endeavors. ME! Inhaling and consuming any substance into your body. ME! Letting anyone have a piece of your soul. ME!

I'm here to tell you that you are chosen. You are not the same as the rest of the world. The devil is working overtime to take you out.

He has tried hundreds of times to take you out. But when God knows he has a purpose and plan that he needs you to fulfill, he will work double-time to pull you out.

He will chastise you. Give you blatant warnings. Speak through animals, babies and trees to get you to understand, my child, you are chosen. Stay focused and don't lose sight. You are almost there.

You're gonna fall off the wagon but don't miss your chance to get back up on the wagon and ride like you never fell off.

I'm here to tell you that was me. I bumped my head. I have disobeyed God. I have done my own thing. I have mistreated myself. I ain't worthy, but because of God's grace and mercy he reminds me that I am chosen. I am an example to others to get it right. Although you will fall short, you can still fulfill your plan and purpose.

Live for Jesus! Let people talk about you! Let people laugh at you. Let people have the last word because when it's all said and done, Jesus done all the above and much more, but he was chosen to die for our sins. And today, we have the chance to get right and have eternal life!

"See now, if I could only get a witness up in here." Bishop exclaims to the congregation.

"Preach it, Bishop Cleveland!" The cathedral yells back.

When you are chosen, you are handpicked to stand out. It feels like you are alone, and that is only because you are different. So you will be alone.

Being chosen means you have to walk a different path. At times, that path will feel alone and cold. Just remember that alone time is your moment to be prepared, shaped, and molded for greatness. Hold on to just a little while longer. You will see why YOU are chosen for greatness.

Everyone cannot walk the path you walk on. Everyone was not built for your passion. YOU are being tailored just for greatness. SO BE GREAT.

Naomi and Bishop Rutherford are speaking to other members at the cathedral about how powerful the message was. How Bishop let the Lord work in and through him. One of the mothers stated that "this is just the beginning, that man is going to be a fire that no man will be able to put out. He sholl gone make a good husband, if I was a couple decades younger."

Bishop Rutherford interrupts her, "Alrighty then, Mother Ballard. Let me get you to the transportation van. You know you do not want to miss the buffet."

"Sholl don't Chile." Mother Ballard pushes her walker quickly to the van.

Naomi walks arm and arm with Bishop Rutherford. They begin to talk about what is on Naomi's mind.

"Bishop Rutherford, can I ask you a question?" Naomi curiously questions.

"Anything sweetie." Bishop Rutherford answers.

"Do you think I will ever have a real relationship with me having all-male best friends? Do you think God shuns down on me fo that?" Naomi continues.

"Goodness, no. You cannot help that your best friends happen to be male. You all are brothers and sisters in Christ first and foremost. We all know there is nothing going on with you and those men. They are great men. Any man that falls in love with you will be truly blessed to inherit a solid brotherhood with them. And no, God does not shun or look down on your friend choice. Be proud of your friends, yourself, your relationship with them, and the way you guide them to the Lord.

All of them are not fully into church, but I can say you have brought each of them on occasions. Those brothers are one of a kind, and so are you, Naomi. So how are things with Bishop? He treating you well?" Bishop Rutherford implies.

"Oh, Bishop Rutherford, come on now. What makes you think we are a thing?" Naomi blushes.

"That right there. Child, the way he looks at you and the way your eyes light up tell it all. You two have been spending more time together at the cafe, he said." Bishop Rutherford over speaks.

"Now, he's going around telling people about me. Great." Naomi says bashfully.

"Don't be shy now. It is nothing wrong with liking someone. Especially after all the negative you had in your life. Plus, I can vouch for my nephew and not just because he is my blood. Because he is a stand-up guy, a go-getter, and a man of God. He likes you a lot, Naomi." Bishop Rutherford states.

"You know. I like him a lot too." Naomi smiles. You can see the butterflies fluttering from the inside out.

"Well, what are y'all waiting for? I am sure God been gave you two a sign. What y'all need a green light?" Bishop Rutherford jokes.

"Bishop!" Naomi shouts with laughter.

"I think I am going to tell him. You know, coming up, it has always been a thing not to let a man know you like or love him first. Let him do the chasing first, they say. I feel that man has been on it from the day one. He never pushed up on me. He just became my friend. He prayed with me and encouraged me. He went on the investors trip and stood by me and the fellas. The fellas like him and my mother loves him. I know my father would have approved of him one hundred times over. I would love to be more with Bishop. I think about a future with him and how we would grow together. I just hesitate when I think about how everything has crumbled in my life. Am I capable of having something good?" Naomi expresses her concern.

"All I can say, Naomi, is pray on it. In the end, it is your decision to let him know or to continue with having a lasting relationship with Bishop. Whatever you decide, just know it is the right decision. Love you, sweetie. Now let me get on down to the buffet. I do not want to miss that smothered fried chicken." Bishop Rutherford rushes to his Cadillac SUV.

Bishop walks over to Naomi.

"Shall we head over to the cafe before your practice?" Bishop questions.

"I thought we would do something different this afternoon. You riding with me." Naomi states.

"Is that a question?" Bishop questions.

"I am telling you that I want you to ride with me. Plus, I am canceling practice today. The girls will be happy to get a break. They said I am killing them for the grand opening." Naomi explains.

"Alright. I am done. So where we heading today? We stepping away from the usual." Bishop asks with curiosity.

"Just sit back and ride." Naomi states.

NAOMI AND BISHOP ARRIVE AT THEIR DESTINATION.

"You can open your eyes." Naomi says.

"I cannot believe you had me ride with my eyes closed the entire time." Bishop jokily complains.

"I did not have a blindfold, and this was spare of the moment. Just could not wait." Naomi says.

"This is absolutely beautiful. How did you find this place?" Bishop questions. As he gets out of the car, he looks around at the scenery.

Walks around to the driver's door and opens it for Naomi. Naomi grabs his hand and walks him to the river. Around the river was art canvased on the flood walls.

"I used to come here every day after school when I came back here. I felt this was the closest to my father and God I was going to get. This river is where my father died. In NOLA, of course. But this river here flows from Saint Louis to New Orleans. Good ole Mississippi River." Naomi explains.

"This means a lot to me, Naomi. Thank you for sharing a piece of the past with me. Why now?" Bishop questions.

"Because I care for you, Bishop. It scares me how much I am falling for you. I do not want to be a fool." Naomi continues.

"Well, I am a fool for you, Naomi Russell. You think you are the only one that has fallen hard. I knew for some time now that you are my person. Then Unc came to me and said, what you waiting on, son." Bishop says.

"Funny. He suggested I not hesitate to tell you my feelings. I did not want to tell you. Most of the time, when women express these types of feelings, the guy runs or just uses the woman." Naomi explains.

"As you must know, I am not your typical man. I do not have the energy to play games with a woman's heart. God put us on this Earth to love our women." Bishop confirms.

"I love how things are going between us and I do not want to rush it. Everything has been flowing so well. You have become one of my best friends." Naomi assures.

"Oh shoot, you just friend-zoned me." Bishop jokes.

"Stop playing. I could never. You are much more. You have become my best friend, confidant, and prayer partner. You are honest, affectionate, a gentleman, appreciative. You demonstrate leadership, trust, and loyalty. Your spirituality is a turn-on to me. Your love for God is a weakness for me. And it is your patience for me." Naomi explains.

"Won't he do it!" Bishop sings.

"Yes, he would!" Naomi sings back.

Naomi and Bishop hug each other and begin to kiss into the sunset. They leave the riverfront in the country and pick up their soul food from the buffet that the entire church goes to. Then they arrive at Bishop's home and they play Scrabble and UNO together.

"You want to read over my sermon scriptures for next week? Maybe even get a prayer in?" Bishop asks.

"Of course. How could I say no to that? Plus, I would be honored to read the honorary Bishop Cleveland's sermon scriptures." Naomi jokes.

Naomi reads over the scriptures as Bishop massages her feet with eucalyptus essential oils. They pray until they feel like they have covered every topic.

"So, it is time to get you back to your vehicle Mr. Cleveland." Naomi says.

"It is late, Ms. Russell. I will catch an Uber in the morning to get it. I just want you to get home safe." Bishop says with a protective tone.

"You are just a gentleman. I am so blessed to call you my man." Naomi giggles.

Bishop walks Naomi to her SUV and watches her drive down the street and she is out of sight.

Naomi texts Bishop.

"I MADE IT HOME. THANK YOU FOR LETTING ME STEAL YOU FOR THE EVENING. BUT IT WAS WELL WORTH IT. WE GOT EVERYTHING OFF OUR CHEST. UNTIL NEXT TIME."

"You are more than worth it. My chest is free and I can now breathe easily. That is until you walk into my view and my chest gets heavy. Until next time, Ms. Cleveland." Bishop replies back.

Bishop places his phone on his nightstand. He stares at the ceiling and prays. He thanks God for the work He has done today, for opening up Naomi's heart and his mind to receive.

Naomi lays her phone next to her, smiles, and begins to thank God. She is in awe at how the day went. She did not expect Bishop to feel the same way she felt. As she begins to doze off, she remembers that she wanted to ask Maggie to meet with her to discuss article ideas.

"MAGGIE. I KNOW IT IS LATE. MEET ME AT THE BAR AND GRILL ON 11TH STREET TOMORROW. 2PM. YOU LOVE HAPPY HOUR, EHHHHH!"

Later she meets up with her supervisor Maggie at a bar and grill to discuss ideas for the next article. Maggie had given Naomi a deadline months ago. It is now going on a year. This is the most lenient she has been with anyone. Mostly due to the fact they are SORO sisters. They both went to a HBCU in Alabama. Maggie took off with the career and now doing the dang thang.

"OO-OPP" Maggie calls out.

Naomi walks up to the bar table and she greets Maggie.

"Hey girl. Come on now. We been out of college too long. You still calling out." Naomi says.

"Hey Naomi. Come on, girl, lighten up." Maggie states in her southern Alabama voice.

"Sorry girl. I just let the SORO life back in 'Bama. I do appreciate you meeting me here and all. Especially on short notice. I want to discuss with you the article that I am typing up now." Naomi continues.

"Yes, we most definitely need to discuss that. Girl, I need a hit article back in 2019. It is a new year. I know you been trying to get investors for the business and the studio launched and all. Any other executive would have let you go when they saw you pursuing other business ventures while working for them. But see, I consider you a friend or at least a close business partner. I know you have several friends, and you not looking for another; well, a woman that is." Maggie says under her breath.

"Excuse me. What does that mean?" Naomi questions in defense.

"I just mean, we was cool in college, but you always seem to cling to men." Maggie points out.

"Hold up one minute, Maggie. I never CLING to men. See, I have always clicked with men because of how negative women can be. This right here is the prime example." Naomi fires back.

"I am sorry, Naomi, I did not mean it like that. All I mean is that it is rare to see a woman around all men and she not smashing them. You know how that went down in college." Maggie reminisces.

They both say, "choot choot."

"Lord forgive us. That was not right." Naomi says a quick prayer.

"Yeah, we was cool in college. You was my girl." Naomi sighs.

"Sholl was. I was a small town 'Bama girl that looked up to the big city STL/NOLA girl. I thought you was the coolest." Maggie rubs Naomi's shoulder with hers.

"Anyways, tell me about your article ideas." Maggie continues to ask.

"So there is this Bishop at Mount Sinai Cathedral. You know that Cathedral has quite a history, of course, we do not talk about it here. The Bishop's name happens to be named Bishop. Funny right. He is quite the gentlemen." Naomi smiles to herself.

"Girl, you looking all in awe and stuff." Maggie notices.

"Stop it, girl. So he can preach the word of God. He is on fire and will preach your socks off." Naomi says.

"Is that right now? I am going to stop by and get the word. Lord knows I need it. Is that fine friend of yours going to be there?"

"Who?" Naomi questions.

"Riq! Silly." Maggie replies back.

"Really, you supposed to be coming to hear the word of God and learn more about the Bishop in training. Girl, let's get back on track. So he wants to give the point of view of being a Bishop in a Catholic setting. Of course many of the catholic rules have not changed. It is different for him coming from a Baptist setting. He and his Uncle Bishop Rutherford, would like to implement changes and convert the cathedral to non-denominational. Of course, that is going to shake some boots and turn some heads. If we can give his viewpoint and some of the members viewpoint about that positive change, then maybe; just maybe that will help the city approve that conversion." Naomi explains.

Maggie ponders for a moment and sips on her margarita.

"So, what do you think? It is too much, isn't it? I know you do not like getting all into religion, but this is huge. Since when you seen a Bishop preaching in a cathedral and changing to non-denominational?" Naomi rambles.

"Well, Naomi. I...I LOVE IT!" Maggie shouts.

"Yes. I knew you would!" Naomi shouts back.

Maggie looks at her with a side-eye and they both laugh.

Chapter 6
Turn Back the Hands of Time

"You can't just stick around and watch me die. I will not let you do that. You are a great man and deserve a woman with no problems and who can give you children. Who you can have a long life with.." Naomi explains.

"Let me stop you right there, Naomi. You do not get to choose my life for me. I chose to stick by your side through this. You just cannot dictate how I cope with your condition. I know I can be with anyone, but I do not know just any woman. I want you. Your heart is real and your soul is pure. There is no other woman I have felt this with. There is no other woman that has prayed for my soul. As if your prayer would be sufficient for my repentance for the love I feel for you. You taught me about agape love, baby. Did you not teach others about agape love?" Bishop cries, begging Naomi hears his heart.

"I understand Bishop, but this is not fair to you. This is not fair. I love you so much and if you are sure you want to stick this out, then I am sure I want to continue this fight with you." Naomi cries out.

"Yes, I am not going anywhere. Naomi Russell, my beautiful, strong, intelligent, queen; will you do be the honor in taking my hand in marriage?" Bishop kneels down at her bedside.

"Really, while I am bawling in my own tears?" Naomi sadly laughs.

"Do not start this again." Bishop laughs.

"Well, Bishop Cleveland. I, I. I do oooh." They both cry, laugh, and hug each other.

"Today is going to be a great day. I finally get to go to the bridal store and choose my dream gown. I had been feeling sick to the bone for weeks. Whoever could have thought, I, Naomi, would be marrying the love of my life?" Naomi gushes with joy.

"I always knew your king was out there, baby. You are too good of a person to have to be alone in this world. Now there is not anything wrong with being alone and getting to know yourself and spend one on one time with God." Naomi's mother states.

"Yes, ma'am, you are right about that. I wish daddy could be here though." Naomi ponders.

"You know he is in your heart, I have not been the best parent and mother to you, but I am forever grateful that God touched your heart to forgive me." Mother exclaims.

"Oh, momma, you are what God gave to me while we are on this Earth. If he can forgive wholeheartedly, so can I." Naomi's mother hugs her tightly.

"You know he would have cried like a baby seeing you in that dress. Bishop would not have a chance to drop a tear." Mother laughs.

They both begin to laugh.

"So are the fellas meeting up with Bishop to get their tux fitted?" Mother questions.

"Should be. What time is it?" Naomi asks, looking around for a clock. Mother looks down at her watch and replies,

"2:00PM."

"They should be there now, let me just text them and see."

Naomi places her phone down on the pearly white plush coach and proceeds to look at herself in the mirror.

The fellas are across town and are meeting up with Bishop to get fitted for tuxedos.

"Welcome gentlemen to Suave Occasions. You must be the lucky groom?" Says the store associate.

"You can definitely say that I am lucky, but I am truly blessed." Bishop states.

His groomsmen and Naomi's bride's men put Bishop on their back and carry him to the fitting area. They place him in front of the large mirrors and large chandelier light fixture.

"Man, I still do not know how Naomi is going to get this to work. No females in the bridal party, you know I got to see some ladies. Flame gone enjoy this." Enrique laughs.

"Do not let Flame hear you play like that, he gone drive you crazy. You think I am bad." Ekon laughs even harder.

Bishop shakes his head at the guys. Flame walks in very excitedly.

"Always fashionable late." Enrique jokes.

"Riq, now you know you are always late to everything. You won't be late to your funeral cause ima personally deliver you." Flame cracks up in laughter.

All the fellas laugh.

"Alright, alright now y'all have had'enough fun, let's get fitted you know Naomi does not want a mess." Bishop states.

All the men begin to grab the tuxedos and proceed to their fitting rooms. Hunter walks out of the fitting room and he notices Bishop is struggling with his bowtie.

"You know for my wedding, Liz wanted me to wear the bowtie I wore on our first date to our wedding." Hunter reminisces.

"You wore a bowtie to your first date and where was you all on your first date?" Bishop questions with a slight laugh.

"It was Go-Kart racing." Hunter pauses in glee.

They both begin to laugh.

"Interesting Hunter." Bishop states.

"You know, brother, I am truly surprised you never asked Naomi if she was feeling for one of us or has been in a relationship with one of us." Hunter inquires.

"No, I have not." Bishop confirms.

"You know she is a beautiful woman inside and out and we all would love a woman with the qualities Naomi possesses. But Naomi would always say there is a special person for each of us." Hunter continues.

"And she is right." Bishop agrees.

He sits down and puts his elbows to his knees and looks up to Hunter.

Bishop continues, "Naomi carries herself differently. When I say differently, that is a good different. I can tell by the way a woman carries herself. I see how she move! Naomi carries herself with grace, morals, and with God first. I can say you brothers are so handsome, educated, and driven. I would not blame her for choosing to love you all in her own way!" Bishop breaks it down to Hunter.

"That right there confirms that I am giving her away to a stand-up guy. You're okay in my book." Hunter proudly says.

They both walk back to their dressing rooms. Bishop is holding his head up to God, pointing and smiling.

Later that evening, Naomi and Bishop meet up for dinner at Bishop's place. Naomi daydreams and Bishop touches her hand.

"Naomi, what is on your mind? You have an uneasy look on your face. Is this moving too fast?" Bishop rambles.

Naomi comes out of the daze.

"No, no, not at all. I am ready, my King. I am very much in love with you. It's just that." Naomi pauses and grabs his hands tighter.

"It's just that my father was my all in this world. He helped me get to where I am today. I wish he could be here for our wedding and you both have the talk. He would give you a hard time at first and ask why you want to marry his daughter." Naomi chuckles softly.

"I spoke to your father." Bishop interjects.

"Don't be silly. What is he alive and you didn't tell me?" Naomi laughs.

"No ma'am. You remember when I told you I had to take a mental health day?" Bishop questions.

"Yesss." Naomi slowly answers.

"Well, I took a day trip to NOLA, and I went to your father's burial site. I sat there and professed my love for you. I told him how much I loved you and how God made you for me. How you are my good thing. I finally asked him if I could take your hand in marriage. I asked him for his blessing." Bishop states.

Naomi holds Bishop's face and places her forehead to his forehead. Naomi cries silently and praises God.

"You know, when I was younger, I dreamt of having the man of my dreams. Never believing that day would come. My reality exceeds that expectation. Thank you, Mr. Bishop Cleveland." Naomi says gratefully.

Chapter 7
The Best Part

It is finally Naomi and Bishop's wedding day. Naomi feels under the weather, sickle cell symptoms are increasing. Her vision is becoming progressively worse. Naomi remembers that vision loss is also a complication of sickle. The thought of not being able to see her future children breaks her heart. She has begun to develop leg ulcers that are manageable for now. Also, the acute chest pains are increasing.

"Probably does not help that my anxiety is through the roof." Naomi says to herself.

She toughs out all the pain because she wants to enjoy every moment of this special day, she waited for in all 36 years of her life.

Naomi's mother walks into the room and helps her sit up in the bed.

"How are you feeling today, baby?" Mother questions.

Naomi looks at her mother with a bothered look on her face. She plays off her emotion with a smile and replies, "Oh, you know me, mama; I am just peachy."

"Baby, you do not have to be strong right now. And you sholl don't have to be strong for anyone in here. You are at the most challenging time of your life. Let someone carry your load for once. I am here now, and I will be here, even when you do not want me there. God placed an amazing man in your life for a reason. He gave you five best friends that will stand and be your support. Let us know when you are not feeling like yourself." Mother pleads.

Naomi begins to cry and then wipes her tears to show that she is still strong.

"Mama, my vision is getting worse. Soon I will not be able to see the people I love. I will not be able to see my children one day. I will not be able to dance with my girls and guide them. I will not be able to see my husband!" Naomi softly explains.

"You know when I walked out of your life, I did not think to myself how I would hurt you. But I did. I hurt you tremendously. You still overcame it all with the help of God and your father. If you endured the pain I caused on your childhood, baby you will conquer this condition; and you have an army behind you. Now come on, baby, and get this beautiful dress on so Hunter can get you down the aisle and your brothers and I can watch you walk gracefully to your soon-to-be King." Mother motivate Naomi.

Mother helps Naomi get dressed, along with her caregiver and stylist. Naomi takes her medicine and it helps her with the pain. She is able to push through the pain for a few hours. Naomi is escorted to the door by Hunter. Hunter gives Naomi the strongest but gentlest hug.

Hunter and Naomi stand in front of double doors that lead to the inside of the cathedral. They interlock arms and the song "All of Me" by John Legend plays as they walk down the aisle. Everyone begins to rise. Naomi gazes at everyone that has come to watch her and Bishop become one. She is filled with joy to see all the people who came out to see their union, her Vanessa girls, congregation members, co-workers, and Bishop's family and close friends. Both Naomi and Hunter finally get to where Bishop is awaiting Naomi. Bishop Rutherford begins the ceremony.

"Who gives this woman to be married to this man?" Bishop Rutherford questions.

All of the guys look at each other and laugh.

"We do!" They all yell out.

"Alright now!" Naomi's mother yells out as well.

Hunter gives Naomi a hug and gives her hand over to Bishop. The ceremony is beautiful and the love demonstrated brought everyone to tears.

As the reception is coming to an end, Bishop proposes a toast to his new bride.

"Mrs. Naomi Cleveland. That has a ring to it." He says proudly.

Everyone laughs.

He holds her hand and helps her stand.

"Today, you made me the most blessed man to walk this Earth, since Jesus Christ himself. Today you became my wife, my helpmate, my rib, the partner, my good thang. I am here for you for the rest of our lives. You cannot get rid of me if you wanted to."

Everyone gathers around to embrace Naomi and Bishop's first dance. They dance to "Happily Ever After" by Case. Naomi is not able to stand for long, so Oletha is able to finish the dance off with Bishop. The fellas assist her back to her designated seat. Naomi sits in bliss and grateful for the blessing she has. Deep down, it is killing her that she is not able to be the woman that Bishop fell in love with. At least that is what she thinks. After everyone devours the delicious meal that Oleatha helped cater, it is time to cut the cake. The cake stood three feet tall with personalized toppers that were cartoon versions of Naomi and Bishop. Embrace that inner child is what Naomi would say.

He swoops Naomi off of her feet and they get into the carriage that awaited. They arrive to the resort (IN AUSTRALIA), where the staff had prepared the most beautiful entrance.

When the newlyweds get to their suite, Bishop sits Naomi down on the California king bed. He gently takes off her slides. Her feet are swollen from the medicine, but he kisses them and begins to massage them. Naomi cries.

Bishop replies, "If this is not the time, I understand. We can wait as long as you need to."

"No baby, I am ready. I have waited patiently on this day. To give myself to my husband, that you are. I am ready, my king." Naomi says softly.

Naomi and Bishop make love for the first time and the passion between them both is divine. Naomi has never felt so much pleasure in her body, to give herself completely to the man of her dreams. Bishop has never been with a woman, who has loved herself wholeheartedly to wait on her husband. Who has love for God and vows to keep herself until marriage? You do not often hear of a woman doing that. Their first time together as husband and wife was magical. In fact, it was more than magical. It was majestic and filled with God's blessing and power. This is the result of faith, patience, perseverance, and obedience.

Naomi and Bishop return to Saint Louis from Australia. They did not want to let go of the beautiful moments they shared together. Bishop and Naomi had to quarantine for fourteen days before they could see their family and friends. Before they could attend church physically. Also, before they can go to their favorite spot, the cafe. Lastly, before Naomi could see a physician. Virtual visits were not cutting it. Her symptoms caused her health to decline faster than expected. Bishop and Oleatha were able to get the physician to see Naomi personally at their home and conduct some tests. The results came back that when Naomi contracted Covid-19, that caused her symptoms to aggressively progress. It is now the final days of Naomi's life. The final days of living in true loves bliss.

Naomi breaks the news to her brothers, asks them to come over to their manor for dinner. Bishop and Oleatha are in attendance. They take it hard.

Finally, the congregation can return to church. The members were able to watch the sermons via zoom and the elderly members were able to call in and listen. Bishop was preaching today. All Naomi could think of is how powerful Bishop's message was going to be and how she wanted to curl up with him when he returned. Although, her condition was getting the best of her. She prayed that she could hold on just a little bit longer. She knew she was ready to leave when God called her, but she was not ready to break everyone's heart, especially her husband, to make him a widower. "Lord, I know this is not about my timing. My duty is almost fulfilled here on Earth. I ask you to give me just a little more of your time. I know I am not worthy, but I need it, Lord, so that I can give my last words to Bishop. I ask you to forgive me for my sins. I thank you for the time you have granted me, thirty-eight years of life. Thank for giving me chance after chance, after chance. Thank you for giving me a stronger relationship with my mother. Thank you for keeping my brothers. I ask you to cover all of my loved ones, oh Lord." Naomi prays prostate on the floor. She begins to cry and write her final words to Bishop.

Naomi leaves a letter on her nightstand for her hospice nurse to give to Bishop when he returns from preaching.

"To my faithful, strong, gentle husband. While we have not had many days together as husband and wife, I am blessed to have had this time with you. You came into my life when I least expected it. I was not looking for a man, which I told you several times but you never pushed a relationship. You became my best friend on all levels. We prayed together, read the word together, and shared our goals and concerns with each other. We fought temptation together. You gave me the experience of fully becoming a woman. You waited for me and never desired another woman. You were patient with me when I was an emotional mess. Most of all, you stuck by my side on my sickbed, the true definition of sickness and health. All of this to say, this pain will not last always. Take your time to grieve over me but do not let this consume you. My not so "typical" best friends are your best friends. Create a brotherhood and bond with them. Let them carry your pain on their shoulders and help them grieve as well. I love you, Bishop Cleveland.

I have one more wish. I ask you to take me back to Australia with our brothers. Let my body free on the ocean. Dress me in that beautiful Canary dress.

Bishop Cleveland, you never let me go, but love again! Keep God first in your life!

Your love forever,

Naomi Russell-Cleveland"

Naomi places the letter in an envelope, seals it, and encloses it with a kiss.

Bishop arrives to their manor. He unlocks the door and is shouting and filled with the Holy Spirit from what he delivered at the cathedral today.

"Naomi, my queen. Your man was on fire today. When I say, I let the Lord move me, I thought I was the wind on a stormy night. Naomi, where you at now?" Bishop says excitedly. The hospice nurse walks out and guides him to his and Naomi's bedroom. Before he can walk in, he gathers his emotions. He opens the large double doors and walks in to see Naomi laying upright on their pillows. As if she was simply asleep, Bishop knew it was not just her sleep. She is now at eternal rest. Bishop goes to the bed and holds Naomi until the ambulance arrives to take her to the hospital.

Bishop cleans her frail deceased body and dresses her for the homegoing ceremony. Flame does her makeup.

The guys work to get the arrangements prepared to fly Naomi to Australia. All of them hold it together for Naomi's mother, who kept it strong for all of them as they watched Naomi deteriorate.

The guys gather around her body and remember all the great times they had with Naomi. As requested by Naomi, she is dressed in a Canary yellow dress. Her hair is wrapped with yellow and white roses.

"You know the best part of Naomi is that no matter what people said about her, it never made her negative. She did not care about what people thought of her. She gave me the confidence to be who I am today. She did not make me feel like I was a criminal or a danger to this world. That is how I felt inside. My mother took the rap for my crime, and I get the chance to live. Naomi continuously explained how that is in God's plan, how to genuinely repent. And to just keep living." Flame walks over to Naomi laid out on a decorated canoe and places a flower on her.

E begins to softly cry and he walks over to the canoe and begins to say his last words.

"Naomi was more than a friend and sister to me. She was not a counselor, but she was my confidant. When I did not know my left from my right, she knew how to get me on track. She kept the guys grounded. Naomi loved my jokes but she taught me everything is not a joking moment. Take time to pray about things, good and bad. This is not goodbye, see you soon Naomi, beomi, fe, fi, Naomi." Ekon blows her a kiss, places a flower on her as well; and walks away. Ekon gathers and assists his brothers with pushing Naomi slowly into the South Pacific Ocean.

Bishop breaks down after Naomi's body departs into the ocean. Seven best friends are there to carry him through this heartbreaking journey. As the guys walk off, "If I Die Young," by The Band Perry begins to play.

Bishop, Flame, Enrique, and Javier walk with each other back to the resort, where their journey began. They all sit at the dining area and celebrate Naomi's life. There is much-needed laughter and crying. All of them sit in with each other until the staff informs them that it is time to shut down the dining area. The staff respectfully gave them more time, for they knew they were all in mourning. All of the guys return to the states, back in STL.

Enrique and E meet up at the cafe and they talk about their differences. E is finally able to express to his brother-in-law what he has been dealing with.

"I am so in love with Monica, it hurts to even tell you this." Ekon explains.

"See, I knew you was cheating on Mon. I told her I would kick your..." Enrique goes in on Ekon.

"Woah, woah, woah, hold up now. She cheating on me Rique. I have been protecting her reputation because I did not know for sure.

Mon had the audacity to come to me and give me all the details right after Naomi passed, talking about that was a wakeup call and she didn't want that on her conscious anymore." E states with pain.

"Dang, bro, say it ain't so. She been getting down like that. This whole time I thought you was out here messing with any woman that will give you the time of day. You know what? She is my sister, but I do not condone how she did you. Nobody deserves that kind of treatment. I wish you would have came to me. I am your brother too." Enrique comforts E.

"You think I could have came to you about this? I barely had a backbone to confront Monica with my gut feeling. I could always step to Naomi about it, though. She would pray with me and tell me to leave it in the hands of the Lord. What am I going to do without her now?" Ekon questions.

"That is what I am here for. What your brothers are here for. Now we have Bishop to stand in with us as well. You know Naomi's spirit lives in and through us. Keep your faith, my brother, and know you and Monica will get through this." Enrique assures Ekon.

"We should pray. Almighty Father, we are coming to you with open arms, thanking you for bringing us together, to put aside our differences. We come together to let go of any ill feelings we had toward each other. Life is too short to have animosity against one another. Enrique is my brother and I have agape love for him. Monica is my wife and I have agape love for her. Although I love her, I do not know what the next step is to heal. But I do know you will order my steps accordingly. I do know Enrique and I will have a better friendship and brotherly bond. Forgive us for all our sins. Walk with us and be our best friend. In Jesus's mighty name. Amen." Ekon closes prayer.

"Amen." Enrique closes prayer as well.

Ekon and Enrique are now on better terms. Naomi would be so proud that these two have put aside their differences. Although she is absent from the body and present with the Lord, she too can see this unity.

Later that day, Ekon arrives at his veterinarian clinic to check on Paulie, his raccoon baby. He asked Monica to meet him at the clinic to talk through their issues. Monica arrives at the clinic.

"E, where you at? You know I really do not like it down here. We could have met at home." Monica says in disgust.

Monica walks through the doors leading to Ekon's office. He has candles, rose petals, chardonnay, the finest cut steak, and r&b music playing.

"Sweetheart, I know you prefer to be anywhere but here. I thought since we had our last discussion, we would try to be away from home and the negativity for once." E says.

"I do not know." Monica looks around.

She then screams when Paulie walks past her feet and hops onto Ekon's desk.

"See, I told you I don't like it down here. If you don't get that rodent away from me this instant!" Monica yells out.

"Mon, when did you become so bitter? It is me, your husband, Ekon." E questions.

Ekon places Paulie in his kennel. He walks over to Monica and gets her down from the desk and sits her in one of the client chairs. She grabs his hands and shakes them.

"You know, I feel you are weak. I just do not see you as an actual physician. For goodness sake, you have a pet raccoon. I thought you would be a neurologist or at least an orthopedic. This don't make no money, baby." Monica laughs.

"But this is my passion. I am in love with what I do. You know what? I am done explaining to you that this is my gift. You of all people should understand. You are my wife." E says as he stands up.

"Was your wife. I filed for divorce when I broke the news to you." Monica heartlessly says.

"That is just fine. I did all I could do. I was a great husband. I loved you unconditionally and still tried to make this work. You shall reap what you have sown. Please leave my establishment." E states as he escorts her to the clinic's main entrance doors. Ekon walks back into his office and chills with Paulie.

"What a night, man. Well, at least I got my little buddy and we can enjoy this fine dinner. How's that sound, Paulie?"

Paulie curls under Ekon and chitters back at him, then begins to purr.

Ekon laughs and enjoys the dinner and music.

On the other side of town. Javier has been spending more time increasing his English vocabulary. He has someone that is taking time with him. That person so happens to be Ms. Thang. Well, that is what they called her at the Life Skills trip in Australia. Her name is actually Scarlet Avery.

Nubia is having a difficult time coping with her Godmother being gone. She stepped in when her mother passed. Hunter tells Nubia that he wishes her mother, Elizabeth and Godmother, Naomi were still with them also, explaining that they are together in heaven now. She has two guardian angels looking after her.

"Guardian angel?" Nubia questions.

"Yes darlin.' A guardian angel is someone handpicked by God to watch over you and protect you while you are on this Earth." Hunter replies.

"God said he loves his children. I am thankful for God loving me. I love him too, daddy." Says Nubia as she hugs her father.

Across town, Flame is learning more about the word of God. He is at the Cathedral for bible study with Bishop Rutherford and the congregation.

Enrique is taking time to work on himself, work on past insecurities and coping with bottled-up feelings. His mother walked away when he was just a young boy. He never knew his father. So, of course, there were some abandonment issues that needed to be dealt with. He hid those feelings with jokes, mainly towards Ekon.

"No wonder we are so messed up. Our mother walked out on us. Our father was nowhere to be found. Our grandmother did the best she could with Monica and me. I know that is no excuse, Lord. But use me in whatever way you need me, Lord. I give myself to you. Change my heart. I also pray that you prepare me for the wife I have longed for. In the name of the Father. Amen."

Enrique prepares himself for a busy few months. It has been hard not having Naomi to lean on. From time to time, he goes to community events and provides free credit counseling. Him being an accountant keeps him busy but not too busy to find love. God will work on his heart, mind, soul, and desires. He knows Naomi would want nothing but the best for him. She always told him, "keep God first and the head of everything you do." Riq did just that.

Conscious Revelation

When Naomi wakes from a dream, screaming and crying, she begins praying and thanking God.

"Thank you for another opportunity at life. I see now that this is not my time to go, but it will be soon. If this was a vision, I am prepared to walk the journey. In Jesus's most precious name, Amen!"

Naomi gets up and gets ready for a morning jog to help ease her mind. As she is running through the park enjoying the beautiful scenery, a man accidentally bumps into her and knocks her down.

"I am so sorry, here let me help you up." Mystery man.

Naomi just stands there while he talks (inaudible sounds).

"Sooo, my name is…"

"Bishop." Naomi knowingly smiles.

"Naomi." Bishop hesitantly says.

And it begins to end!

Acknowledgments

First we would like to give all honor to God who is truly the head of our lives. Without allowing God to lead and guide us, getting through this journey called life would be impossible. God has given us a purpose and daily we try to get closer to that purpose.

We thank our family that have transitioned to be with the Lord. Your encouragement resonates with us now more than ever. Thank you to all the family who we have living, and breathing is this world; far and near. Thank you for motivating us with your words, prayers, and unconditional love.

Also, to our outstanding friends who drive us to be the best women that we can be. We appreciate our photographer for our amazing photoshoots. Pastor Savage and First Lady Savage, we are forever grateful for your time, dedication, and love for the Lord. LaSalle Baptist will Always be Home.

Our beautiful children and grandchildren: Michela Alexander, Teygan Brown, Teyana Brown, A'miya Tyler, Kenzie Ward, and Keelan Ward. The reason we are striving to be the beacons for our generational wealth is because of you six! Just know there is nothing you cannot accomplish. Keep God first always! Never give up!"

Let us embark on a journey to learn about the authors. These authors are two phenomenally strong women. Both have a story like everyone in this world. The women have chosen to demonstrate that even though the paths are similar, the end goal is to break generational curses. Asia and Lefornia Martin welcome you to a reality of growth.

Asia Martin is Founder of AsIAm Studios, LLC. Her hometown is Saint Louis, Missouri and loves to travel. Asia has five amazing children and loves to explore with them. Also, she encourages them to write out their creative thoughts. She believes people have the ability to be who they are, love themselves, and embrace life. Asia has begun the writer journey by watching her mother build her own production company. Her mother is the second author of "The Best Part of Her." Also, has an associates in Business Administration (Entrepreneurship).

Currently is pursuing her Bachelors in Producing. She is striving to work with notable and creditable experts in the entertainment industry. Asia is a brain aneurysm survivor, and she hosts local walks and runs.

Lefornia Martin is Founder of Aja Mango Production Company/ Jed Muddy Uptown Dining Theater. She believes that people should always think bigger to achieve goals, so that they can reach their highest potential. Be a person that does not have to depend on others. Always live what you speak out of your mouth. There is nothing wrong with growing from your mistakes. Lefornia has a Bachelors in Sports Entertainment Management. She is currently pushing through the master program and majoring in Special Education (SPED). Lefornia has written scripts for screenplays and is currently working on a memoir about her breast cancer journey. She is family-oriented and enjoys giving back to others.

Thank you for taking the time to understand the authors. There will be more to come from Asia Martin and Lefornia Martin.

www.ingramcontent.com/pod-product-compliance
Lightning Source LLC
Chambersburg PA
CBHW031031190726
48286CB00003BA/1119